Bruce began to tremble when he looked up at the gorgeous girl who stood before him with a roguish smile on her pretty face. His eyes widened as he realised that Rosie had taken off all her clothes and was standing naked except for a shiny semi-transparent robe through which he could see the dark mounds of her nipples and the outline of the thick pubic muff between her thighs.

'Well, does sir like what he sees or shall I parcel up the merchandise again?' she asked coquettishly, but Bruce swiftly regained his composure and he replied thickly: 'I'll take everything you have in stock – and please let me finish unwrapping the goodies.'

'Be my guest,' said Rosie sweetly. She sat herself down on Bruce's thighs and threw her arms around him as he kissed her full on her rich, red lips. She responded eagerly and her tongue slid wetly inside his mouth whilst Bruce cupped the firm rounded globes of her breasts in his hands, squeezing the large hardening nipples . . .

Summer School 3: Hot to Trot

Dick Rogers

NEW ENGLISH LIBRARY
Hodder and Stoughton

First published in 1994 by Hodder and Stoughton
A division of Hodder Headline PLC
A New English Library paperback

A CIP catalogue record for this title
is available from the British Library

ISBN 0 450 60170 6

Typeset by
Letterpart Limited, Reigate, Surrey

Printed and bound in Great Britain by
Cox & Wyman Ltd, Reading

Hodder and Stoughton Ltd
A division of Hodder Headline PLC
338 Euston Road
London NW1 3BH

This is for Sheena Walshaw and Sally Randall,
two jolly good sports.

Why, one makes lovers as fast as one pleases,
and they live as long as one pleases, and they die
as soon as one pleases: and then if one pleases,
one makes more
William Congreve [1670–1728]

Chapter One

Business With Pleasure

Denise Cochran yawned as her eyes fluttered open. She looked down at the tousled blonde head which was lying in the crook of her shoulder. The perfume from the girl's hair came up to her nostrils and she rubbed her cheek against its silky softness.

'Sharon, are you awake? We both have to make an early start,' she whispered. But the girl only shifted within the circle of her arms like a sleepy kitten. 'M'mmm, just give me five more minutes, there's a darling,' she purred. Denise sighed and said: 'Oh, all right, but not a second more than five minutes. It's almost a quarter past seven – I'm sure you haven't forgotten how angry Dr Teplin was when you were late last Tuesday morning.'

'Sod the old bugger,' mumbled Sharon. Denise smiled sympathetically and kissed her on the forehead. She too would have loved nothing better than another delicious hour of slumber. Like the younger girl, Denise was still tired from the effects of their wild session of lesbian love-making the previous night, which had lasted into the early hours.

However, Denise wanted to scan her notes one final time before the ten o'clock seminar with Dr Bruce Teplin, the sharp-tongued lecturer in business studies at

Falmington-On-Sea's College of Higher Education summer courses. Sharon Shaw was Dr Teplin's secretary and her blonde bed-mate knew full well how the lecturer from the London School of Economics prided himself on working at maximum efficiency. He would be most annoyed if, for the second time in a week, Sharon was not in his office at nine fifteen sharp, shorthand notebook in hand and ready to take down his dictation.

She looked down at the firm curves of Sharon's perky little breasts and licked her lips as she slid her hands over the teenage girl's high-tipped titties, rolling them around on her palms until they stiffened up like two red rubbery bullets and Sharon offered no resistance as Denise started to squeeze the soft hillocks of her bosoms.

'Ooooh, don't do that or I'll never get out of bed,' she muttered when she felt Denise's lips close upon her right nipple and begin to suck, tenderly at first and then with a heightened urgency as her fingers moved into the silky muff of fluffy hair which fringed Sharon's pretty pussy. 'You naughty thing,' she added as Denise slipped her index fingers between the pouting pussy lips, moving them expertly inside her love funnel whilst the heel of her hand rubbed against her clitty which was now as hard as a little walnut.

Sharon let out a tiny sigh and raised up her bottom from the sheet to enjoy to the very utmost the sensations afforded by this finger-fuck. Their bodies writhed from side to side in an orgy of erotic glee despite her misgivings about the lack of time. Sharon whispered huskily: 'Don't stop now, darling. You must finish me off!' Denise swiftly hauled herself on top of her and pressed against Sharon's quivering body. Her forefinger was now embedded in the other girl's tingling quim whilst her velvet tongue slithered between Sharon's lips. She slid a third finger into the teenager's juicy love box.

'Aaargh! Aaargh!' she panted with feline pleasure as Denise's fingers danced in and out of her cunt whilst she moved her head downwards to the damp pleasure patch of pubic hair. Then Denise replaced her fingers with the tip of her tongue as she grasped the dimpled cheeks of Sharon's bum, one jouncy buttock in each hand as she planted a passionate kiss directly on to her cunt, her mouth fused against the soft, yielding flesh as she delicately probed the pink crack with her tongue.

Denise inhaled the pungent cuntal aroma and closed her eyes whilst she flashed the tip of her pointed tongue between the rolled love lips. She licked and lapped inside Sharon's sopping sheath, sucking and swallowing the love liquid which was freely flowing into her mouth. 'I want to cum as well,' she whispered as she removed one hand from Sharon's backside and began to frig her own pussy which was already dripping wet with the evidence of her own arousal.

But this didn't matter at all to Sharon, who gurgled happily: 'Yes! Yes! I'm almost there!' She started to shake with excitement as Denise's tongue swept over the walls of her cunny. Her hips bucked violently in a frenzied rhythm as she orgasmed with a fierce shriek and flooded Denise's mouth with a burst of pussy juice before collapsing back on to the mattress.

'Now it's my turn,' gasped Denise as she finger-fucked herself at an ever-increasing speed until, with a heartfelt little cry, she achieved her release and slumped back beside Sharon's inert body.

They lay quite still for two or three minutes and Denise wondered whether it had been the fresh seaside air that had caused her to become consumed by this sudden lustful need to make love to the delectable eighteen-year-old girl, who had already lapsed back again into a sleepy doze.

It was not as if Falmington-On-Sea enjoyed the same nudge-nudge reputation as Brighton, the far better known and larger resort which lay some twenty miles or so to the east, although it was true that back home in London she shared a flat and her bed with a pretty if promiscuous teenage beauty named Jenny Forsyth. But Jenny was without doubt bi-sexual with a growing propensity to spend at least two nights a week with her ruggedly handsome boss and after a quick but passionate fling with Murray Lupowitz, a young American who was working temporarily in her office, Denise was rapidly coming round to the conclusion that her own lesbian tendencies were also on the wane.

These tendencies had first shown themselves at boarding-school when her 'pash' on the captain of hockey had led to her being seduced by the older girl who had pulled down her knickers and tickled her pussy up to orgasm in the dormitory after lights out. There had followed some exciting gropes at a party with her best friend's brother, but Denise's lesbian feelings had later been furthered at Cambridge University. Here, during her first year, she had lost her virginity to her first serious boy friend. But the experience had been shambolic, a quick sixty-second knee-trembler against the walls of Trinity College and she had eagerly responded to the sensual advances of one of her female tutors.

However, Denise and Murray Lupowitz had enjoyed several torrid nights together in his bedroom at the Berkeley Hotel* even though neither of them were in Falmington on holiday. Murray had enrolled on a crash course in Spanish at the town's noted College of Higher Education before he went to work on an assignment in

* See 'Summer School I, Warm Days, Hot Nights' [New English Library]

4

South America and Denise was spending three weeks there on a business studies course, by courtesy of her employers, the old established publishers Chelmsford and Parrish for whom she had been worked as an editorial assistant since leaving Cambridge with a first-class honours degree in English Literature.

Not surprisingly, she had hardly jumped for joy when George Radlett, Chelmsford and Parrish's editorial director, had first suggested that she enrolled for a business management summer school course. For this was to be Denise's reward after she had discovered a brand new writer whose novel, *A Delightful Scandal*, she had not only rescued from the pile of uncommissioned manuscripts which were often sent back unread, but had then somehow managed to pilot the raunchy novel past the objections of the company's staid, ultra-cautious chairman, a feat which everyone else in the editorial offices speculated would earn them all a handsome Christmas bonus as it was confidently expected that *A Delightful Scandal* would be a huge bestseller.

However, Denise was frankly disappointed when, instead of a pay rise, all George Radlett had offered her was an all-expenses-paid three weeks of study at Falmington-on-Sea. 'These days, you can't simply sit round the table and discuss the literary merits of this or that author,' George had said earnestly to Denise whose gloomy face showed her initial reaction to the idea. 'This is 1967, my love, and editors are expected to be hands-on executives, able to read balance sheets just as thoroughly as general fiction – although in my experience there isn't all that much difference between the two!

'Anyhow, if you want promotion either here or at any other publishers, I strongly recommend you snap up this chance to widen your business skills and pop down to Falmington this summer.'

So Denise had taken George Radlett's advice and signed up for the course. As it turned out, the experience was not quite so boring as she had feared. For the first week she had been buoyed by her nightly fucks with Murray Lupowitz and she felt a familiar tingle in her groin when she thought of the warm waves of ecstasy which had rippled through her body when he had inserted the wide mushroom dome of his circumcised cock between her pussy lips. She was tempted to slide her fingers into her quim to try and recapture those glorious sensations but then she glanced at the bedside clock and firmly banished such enticing thoughts from her mind.

'Come on, lazybones, it's time to get up,' she said briskly as she pinched the blonde girl's bottom. 'If we don't make a move we'll have to fork out for a taxi to get us to the college by nine fifteen.'

If she had but known where Dr Bruce Teplin had stayed the night, Denise would not have worried about being late for her morning seminar. For to his great delight, Bruce Teplin had finally accomplished his objective of bedding the tutor in social sciences, the glamorous Miss Rosie O'Hara, beating off a challenge from Dr Edwin Radleigh, the Principal of the College and several other competitors including Falmington-On-Sea's publicity officer, the former Fleet Street journalist, Bernie Gosling who had the unenviable job of trying to persuade the great British public to ignore the charms of the new, cheap package holidays to the guaranteed sunshine coasts of Italy and Spain and spend a more traditional two weeks in the more bracing climate of West Sussex.

But this was a time of triumph for Bruce Teplin. The wheel of good fortune had begun to spin in his direction the previous afternoon. To trace the path which led to his first passionate embrace with the luscious Rosie O'Hara, it will be necessary to put back the clock to the previous afternoon in the college library . . .

It had been a hard afternoon's work for Bruce, who had to deliver a sixty-minute lecture on trade union law to his class. Then he planned to closet himself in the library and correct the proofs of his new book on the need for more flexible industrial management structures when Britain finally joined the European Common Market. So, after the students had filed out of the room, he hurried along to the library and sorted through the pages which his publisher had asked him to read through as soon as possible. This was his first book and Bruce found it curiously satisfying to see his typed manuscript in print. He read through each page carefully, making a clutch of minor corrections as instructed with a red ball-point pen.

Nevertheless, it was tiring work, and at half past four Bruce decided to take a short break from his labours. He rose from his desk and ambled to the door. Then, as he was about to pull it open, he saw Rosie O'Hara put back a book on the shelves and walk towards him. Not for the first time, Bruce admired her pretty oval face, large dark eyes and the generous wide lips which were made even more striking by a liberal application of a bright red lipstick.

He held open the door for her and Rosie smiled as she passed by him and then turned back and said: 'Hello there, Bruce, I'm on my way to the canteen – can I tempt you with a fairy cake and a cup of coffee?'

With difficulty, he tore his eyes from her full, rounded breasts which swelled so seductively under her cream-coloured blouse. I would be tempted to walk down to the canteen on my hands and knees for a squeeze of those lovely boobs, he thought to himself, as he cleared his throat and answered: 'Yes, thank you, that would be lovely, only let me take you round the corner to Claire Café in Moser Street. She actually makes real coffee as opposed to the cheap supermarket instant served up in the canteen. And if you can resist her chocolate cake, you're a better man than I am, Gunga Din!'

'Oh ho, do I detect a romance in the air? Doctor Radleigh was asking for some new stories for the College Magazine,' she laughed whilst they walked through the main College doors and down the steps to the pavement. Bruce shook his head and said solemnly: 'Only between me and Claire's cake, I promise you. I know they say that the way to a man's heart is through his stomach, but as Claire is a happily married grandmother, be warned that if you write anything about us other than that she and I are just good friends, you'll very quickly receive a communication from m'learned friends!'

'Don't even mention those rogues,' groaned Rosie with great feeling as they walked across the road and turned into Moser Street. 'My last boyfriend was a solicitor and after my rotten experience in the hands of the law, Bruce, I'm never going even to look twice at any guy with legal connections ever again, let alone accept a date from one.'

They sat down at one of the small tables outside the café and Bruce nodded sagely. 'People have never taken to lawyers,' he agreed with a sympathetic grunt. 'According to Shakespeare, when Jack Cade took up arms against Henry VI he said: "The first thing we do, let's kill all the lawyers!" Perhaps he wrote that when Anne Hathaway had a few problems with the conveyancing of her cottage in Stratford on Avon!'

A buxom middle-aged lady came bustling out of the cafe to take their order and Rosie said gravely: 'A *cappuchino*, please and as I've heard such wonderful things about your chocolate cake, I'm seriously thinking

8

about ordering a slice, but to be honest, I'm worried about the calories.'

'You've no need to worry about your weight, a lovely girl like you,' beamed the waitress as she winked at Bruce Teplin. 'Believe me, dear, most men prefer girls with a few nice curves on them, not like those stick-insects you see in all the fashion magazines. They've got nothing you can grab hold of between the sheets. Anyhow, our chocolate cake has a magic formula and it doesn't contain a single calorie. You have my word on it.'

'H'mm, maybe so but I doubt if that would stand up at the Old Bailey! Still, I suppose I'd better try a piece and find out for myself,' grinned Rosie, but the waitress wagged her finger and said: 'Oh, it's true enough, you can eat a nice thick slice of this cake and then if you take your boy-friend upstairs for a snog, I guarantee you'll burn off all the calories in the cake and more besides!'

She cackled loudly at her own joke whilst Bruce ordered a slice of chocolate cake and an *espresso* coffee. Then, after she had waddled back inside the cafe, Rosie smiled roguishly at her fellow lecturer and remarked: 'I don't know about burning off the calories from her chocolate cake, but I really must start doing some exercise. My flat's less than a quarter of a mile away from the college and in our kind of job we're sitting on our backsides all day. That's the only thing I miss about Colin, my ex-boy friend, the solicitor and shit of the year. We used to play tennis with a couple of friends at least twice a week after work, but since we split almost two months ago, I haven't played more than half a dozen times.'

'I'll be pleased to give you a game,' said Bruce promptly. 'You'll probably knock spots off me, but I could also do with some exercise. Tell me though, Rosie, are you really over this chap? To be honest, it sounds to me as if you're still hurting.'

Rosie looked at him straight in the eye and answered frankly: 'You're right, of course, Bruce, I have to admit that I still miss him a bit – and not just as a tennis partner either! What was more important was that we really turned each other on in bed. Well at least I thought we did, but then I found out that he was cheating on me.'

'Oh dear,' said Bruce, blushing slightly as the waitress returned with two enormous slices of rich-looking chocolate cake which she plonked down in front of them. 'I'm sorry, Rosie, I didn't mean to pry.'

'No, that's okay, it's all in the past,' she said, letting her hand rest momentarily upon his arm before she picked up her fork and transferred a piece of cake to her mouth. 'M'mm, no wonder you come here for a break, this cake really is delicious. Anyhow, about Colin, we didn't break up just because he fucked another girl. I wouldn't have been deliriously happy if I had known he was poking his secretary, though I wouldn't have minded all that much because we weren't living in each other's pockets and were both seeing other people occasionally. No, it was his dishonest behaviour which made me break up with him.'

Bruce saw the waitress coming to the table with their coffees and waited till she had left before he said quietly: 'Well, whatever Colin did, it must have been quite dreadful to make you so angry. Look, if you prefer, we'll change the subject here and now, but I'm happy to listen if you want to tell me more about what happened.'

'Oh, I don't mind talking about it,' Rosie replied with a wry smile. 'In fact, I'd like to hear whether you think I was justified in giving Colin the order of the boot. Funnily enough, it all happened after a party for new members at his tennis club. Colin had telephoned to ask me if he could meet him there as he was going to have to work late. No problem, I said, and then he added that one of his articled clerks who lived near him and was also a member of the club had asked him if he could give her a lift there.

'I guessed this had to be Juliet for I had always thought that this girl fancied him, but this didn't bother me over-much because it was Colin himself who always insisted that we should never start anything going with anyone at work. "You must never mix business with pleasure," he insisted when I told him how I fancied fucking a rather dishy sociology tutor I had met at a conference, so I didn't take up the dinner invitation this guy made in a letter to me a few days later.

'Anyhow, he turned up at the club with her and being on the committee, he had to circulate. I noticed that Juliet always seemed to be at Colin's side, though I still didn't think there was anything between them, even when she tagged on afterwards when a group of us went back to Colin's house in Clerkenwell for a nightcap. There must have been about a dozen or so people there, not all in couples. Whilst I was in the kitchen I was talking to a nice chap from the BBC contracts department who was telling me some funny stories about some of the stars. We continued chatting after he had helped me bring in the coffee to the lounge, but about ten minutes later, he looked at his watch and said he had better be off as he had an early start in the morning.

'I looked round for Colin but I couldn't see him anywhere. When I went upstairs onto the dark landing, I saw a light coming from his bedroom – the door had been left slightly ajar. I was about to push it open when I heard the bed creak and it didn't take Sherlock Holmes to detect that a couple were having it away in there.

'Now, believe me, Bruce, I wouldn't have peered in if I hadn't heard Juliet's voice murmur something like:

11

"Oooh, you are a wicked boy, Colin." You can hardly blame me, can you?'

Bruce Teplin shook his head and let out a sigh.' No, of course not. I'm surprised you didn't just barge in and interrupt the proceedings then and there.'

'I almost did,' she replied with the ghost of a smile. 'But instead I just sidled in and stood in the doorway whilst I watched Colin and Juliet rolling around on the bed. He had taken off her blouse and whilst they were kissing he undid her bra and yanked it off her shoulders. Then she lay back and he began kissing her big red nipples whilst he slid his hand underneath her mini skirt and tugged down her knickers. Then he unzipped his trousers and pulled out his cock whilst she took off her skirt and spread her legs and whispered: "Go on, Colin, fuck the arse off me. It's okay, I'm on the Pill".'

'She knew what she wanted all right,' commented Bruce as Rosie sipped her coffee and went on: 'I'll say she did. She took hold of Colin's cock and said: "Do you mind if I ride you? I fancy being on top tonight. Just lie back and relax, lover, and let me do all the work."

"Be my guest," he said as he rolled over on to his back and as Juliet sat astride him and placed the tip of his knob between her pussy lips he added with a smirk: "Feel my balls, Julie, they're so heavy that I know I'm going to shoot a tremendous load of sticky spunk into your juicy little twat."

"Yes, that's the ticket, Colin, you know I love it when you talk dirty to me," she gasped. It was plain this was by no means the first time that he had fucked her. "But we'd better make it a quickie because Rosie will probably start to look for us if we don't make an appearance downstairs soon. So cream my cunny quickly, you randy sod, but not before I've enjoyed the feel of your thick cock sliding in and out of my cunt for at least a couple of minutes."

'With that she began to slide up and down on his twitching tool, slowly at first and then faster and faster until she was bouncing up and down on his prick at terrific speed. Colin groaned and he clutched her chubby bum cheeks as she leaned forward to let the edge of his knob rub against her clitty as she pushed up and down, squeezing his thighs with her knees and then he gasped: "Christ, I'm coming, my cock's filling up and I can't hold back!"

'He gave an almighty groan as he jetted his jism inside her. She sat still on his cock, relishing the sensation to the full whilst her pussy flooded with a mix of his seed and her own love-juices.

"Sorry if I came too quickly, Julie," he apologised as she rolled off him and propped herself up on an elbow whilst she traced a pattern on his wet shaft with her fingernail. "But that was the most wonderful fuck and I simply couldn't hold on any longer."

"That's all right, just so long as you weren't dreaming about Rosie O'Hara whilst we were on the job," she said. And – now listen to this – do you know what that bastard replied?'

Bruce puffed out his cheeks as he expelled a deep breath before replying: 'Not in so many words, but from the expression on your face, I guess it must have been something absolutely horrific.'

'I'll say it was,' continued Rosie grimly. 'He bent forward and as he kissed her, he said: "Don't be daft, it's you that's in my mind when I'm fucking Rosie, you silly girl." I was so angry that I nearly stormed in to confront Colin and his tart, but it would have been undignified to have made a scene, especially with all those people downstairs.'

'Quite right, there's no point washing dirty linen in public,' Bruce agreed. He paused for a moment and then went on: 'I'm not taking Colin's side, far from it, but I think there's a lot of sense in an old Yiddish proverb which a Jewish chum of mine is fond of quoting to me. Roughly speaking, it says that when a man's cock swells up, his common sense flies out of the window. There's no excuse for what he said for, if he was telling the truth, then you don't want him in your bed. But if he were just saying it to keep Julie happy, then he's a lying toad who also deserves to be kicked into touch.

'All I would ask of you is not to think that all men would behave like that,' he concluded firmly. 'I bloody well wouldn't if I had the luck to date a beautiful girl like you.'

A wide smile flashed across Rosie's face as she finished her coffee and put down her cup. 'Oh, are you telling me that your friend's clever little maxim about stiff cocks doesn't apply to you?' she enquired, with an amused glint in her large dark eyes.

'Ouch! Hoist with my own petard,' said Bruce as he held up his hands in mock surrender. 'Yet I stand by what I said, Rosie, I really do.'

She looked at him carefully and then smiled again as she said: 'Well, in that case, why haven't you ever asked me out?'

'Why haven't I asked you out?' he repeated. Looking down at the garish red tablecloth he muttered: 'Because you're the youngest tutor on the summer school courses and I convinced myself that I wouldn't have a chance to compete with the young men in and around the College.'

Rosie frowned and said: 'Hey, what's the matter with you, Bruce? You're only in your early thirties, aren't you?'

'Thirty-three,' he admitted and she wagged a reproving finger at him. 'That's hardly ancient, is it? I'm twenty-four and Colin and the boy friend before him were also in

14

their thirties. I've been dating older men since I turned twenty-one. Come on, admit it, you were just terrified of being turned down.'

'I can't deny it,' Bruce admitted as he signalled to the waitress to bring the bill. 'Although it wasn't just shyness, the fact is that I would have put serious money on your having a regular boy-friend.'

'No wonder they call economics the dismal science,' she said promptly. 'Anyhow, now you know I don't have a boy-friend in tow, what are you going to do about it, h'm?'

Bruce looked up and said decisively: 'I'm going to ask you out to dinner tonight, Rosie O'Hara, that's what I'm going to do. There's a new Spanish restaurant behind the Berkeley Hotel which has just opened up and it's supposed to be very good. I'll book a table for eight thirty, if I may.'

'You certainly may, kind sir. I like a man who knows his own mind,' she said, graciously inclining her head. 'Come round to my place first for a drink at eight o'clock. Do you have my address, Bruce? It's the garden flat, thirty-six Alexandra Road. We'll only be a five minute cab ride away from the Berkeley.'

They stood up as the waitress came over and after glancing at the bill Bruce pulled out a ten shilling note and plonked it on her saucer without even looking at the bill. 'Keep the change,' he said gaily as he followed Rosie out back towards the college.

'Thank you sir, you're a real gent,' the waitress called out after them as she pocketed the money. 'I hope you'll enjoy burning off the calories from the chocolate cake tonight!'

Unlike most wishes, this one was to be granted for the evening could hardly have gone better. Rosie looked stunning in a green taffeta dress whilst at the restaurant,

Senor Gento's chef excelled himself and produced such a magnificent paella costa Levante that even Bruce, who had a hearty appetite, abandoned the idea of ordering anything except a fresh fruit salad from the sweet trolley.

However, he was more than happy to agree when Rosie suggested that they skipped coffee and went back to her flat instead. 'I've yet to open the bottle of Remy Martin that's been sitting in the cupboard since I arrived in Falmington last month,' she said as Bruce took a final sip of his dry white wine. 'And you can have coffee if you want, but I'm going to make myself a nice cup of tea. Funny, isn't it, that's something you can never get after a meal in a posh restaurant.

'Still, this place is a real find, Bruce, the food was wonderful. Look here though, it was jolly expensive, the set menu was two guineas a head. I don't suppose you'd let me——'

'No, I certainly wouldn't,' Bruce cut in sharply as he counted out the pound notes from his wallet but, correctly thinking that Rosie would like to make even a small financial contribution to the evening, he added: 'Mind, if you have a two shilling piece in your bag, I'll take it from you. I want to leave a little extra something for the waiter but I don't have any small change.'

'Yes, I'm sure I have,' she said as she opened her bag and triumphantly brought out a half-crown coin which she slid across the table to him. She squeezed his hand as he picked it up. They held hands in the taxi back to her flat and they were still holding hands until Rosie had to rummage through her bag again for her keys.

Once inside, she took Bruce's coat and then gestured for him to go into the lounge. 'Take a seat, Bruce and I'll be with you in a minute or two. This dress is for special occasions and as I didn't spill any wine or drop a piece of paella in my lap, I think I'll quit while I'm ahead! So cliché or nor, I'm just going to change into something more comfortable,' she said as she shepherded him inside. 'Make yourself at home, I won't be long,' she added. As if in a dream, he followed her instructions and slipped off his jacket before slopping down into an armchair as Rosie shut the door behind him.

The lonely lecturer's heart began to thump when he realised that he was now within fingertip-reach of the glorious prize he had lusted after since he had first set eyes on the lovely Rosie O'Hara, though it suddenly crossed his mind that there were no certainties in these situations. It was possible that Rosie was only one of those frustrating prick teasers. He gnawed his lower lip when his brain questioned whether he might have mis-read Rosie's body-language signals and far from prepar-ing herself for sex, she was simply changing her clothes for the simple reason she had just given him.

So should he follow his instincts and sweep her into his arms when she reappeared, or play it cool and feign a if-you-want-me-you-must-make-the-first-move attitude. It was vital to choose the right approach because a wrong move now could spoil everything . . .

He hunched forward in the chair and covered his face with his hands whilst he wrestled with this perplexing problem. He did not hear the soft tread of Rosie's footsteps when, as she had promised, she came back into the room only a few minutes later.

However, his head instantly jerked up when he felt Rosie's hand on his shoulder. He heard her say in a soft, amused voice: 'Oh Bruce, I hope you weren't going to sleep without first giving me a good-night kiss.'

Bruce Teplin began to tremble when he looked up at the gorgeous girl who stood before him with a roguish smile on her pretty face. His eyes widened as he realised that Rosie had taken off all her clothes and was standing naked except for a shiny semi-transparent robe through which he could see the dark mounds of her nipples and the outline of the thick pubic muff between her thighs.

'Well, does sir like what he sees or shall I parcel up the merchandise again?' she asked coquettishly, but Bruce swiftly regained his composure and he replied thickly: 'I'll take everything you have in stock – and please let me finish unwrapping the goodies.'

'Be my guest,' said Rosie sweetly. She sat herself down on Bruce's thighs and threw her arms around him as he kissed her full on her rich, red lips. She responded eagerly and her tongue slid wetly inside his mouth whilst Bruce cupped the firm rounded globes of her breasts in his hands, squeezing the large hardening nipples.

'Hold on a second,' she murmured throatily as she pulled his hands away. For a moment Bruce looked startled, but then he gasped as she unbuttoned the robe and wriggled her arms out of the sleeves and her glorious nude body was in his arms. 'Sorry, I know you wanted to take it off but——'

'It doesn't matter,' he gasped as he covered her lips for a second time, driving his tongue between her teeth whilst Rosie's fingers strayed down to his lap. She deftly unzipped his flies, plunging her hand inside to grasp his hot, vibrant cock which had sprung out through the slit of his boxer shorts to display itself naked and throbbing with unslaked desire.

Then as her fist closed around the hot shaft and began to slide slowly up and down the rock-hard fleshy column, Bruce broke off their kiss. He stared at her lush, swaying breasts for a second before he buried his head between them, nuzzling his face against their softness and turning his head from side to side to nibble on each raised red nipple in turn.

He slid his hand between Rosie's legs and she moaned

softly as he set his palm firmly on her bushy mound. He splayed his fingers inside her moist silky bush through which he could feel her rolled pussy lips and the pulsing little clitty which twitched under his touch.

The first trickle of love juice now seeped out of Rosie's aroused cunt and she panted with lust as Bruce rubbed his thumb in a sensuous circular movement against the stiff bud of her excited clitty before plunging inside her juicy quim. She pressed herself down to impale herself upon it as a delicious wave of sensuous delight spread through every fibre of her body.

'I want you to fuck me in bed,' Rosie whispered hoarsely as, with one hand still wrapped tightly around his swollen cock, she slid off his lap to enable Bruce to rise up from the chair. Then she threw her free arm around his neck as he carried her out into the hall and through into her bedroom.

He laid her gently on the bed and climbed between her legs as she lay back, opened her legs and pulled his straining shaft towards the warm, wet haven which awaited it.

Bruce watched her hand slide to and fro along his thick, veined shaft as he moved towards her. She guided him home, easing in the uncapped purple helmet between her pouting pussy lips. He paused for a moment to let the muscles of her love funnel accommodate his width before propelling his prick forward until he was fully embedded inside her and his balls nestled against her spread bum cheeks.

'Aaah! Aaah! That's divine, darling, I feel so full!' she breathed in his ear as he rested his head in the nook of her shoulder. 'Now I want you to summon up all your strength and give me a good fucking, you lovely big-cocked boy!'

'Your wish is my command,' Bruce whispered as he

pulled all but the tip of his knob out of Rosie's dripping honeypot. Then he drove the full length of his throbbing tool fully inside her cunt and began to pump rapidly in and out of her juicy cunny channel. His balls slapped against her backside as she urged him on, swinging her long legs over his back and drumming a tattoo against his spine to force even more of his cock inside her as she thrust her hips upwards to meet his fierce downward plunges.

'Come with me, lover, come with me!' shrieked Rosie when she felt the rapid onset of her orgasm and Bruce thrust his quivering cock inside her clinging quim one final time as he spurted a fountain of sticky seed inside her sopping wet quim which triggered her climax. Their bodies were now drenched with perspiration as, caught in mutual passion, they rocked from side to side until the convulsions finally subsided and they lay trembling in each other's arms.

'Wowee! What a glorious fuck,' sighed Rosie brightly as she heaved herself up and switched on an old-fashioned radio which was perched precariously on the bedside table. 'You don't mind if we have some music, do you? Some girls like to listen to music whilst they make love, but I don't because if I hear one of my favourite songs whilst I'm making love I lose my concentration and begin listening to the lyrics.

'Afterwards though, I find it very relaxing,' she continued as the set warmed up and the sounds of The Rolling Stones filled the room. Bruce looked at her wordlessly with a wry grin which made her giggle as she added: 'Well, as far as the Stones are concerned, it simply doesn't matter because I always feel sexy when I think about Mick Jagger!'

'Yes, there's something primeval about bands like The Rolling Stones which attracts woman like kids to the Pied

Piper,' Bruce agreed as he ran his fingers lightly over the damp curly patch of hair which covered Rosie's delectable pussy. 'Mick Jagger, John Lennon, and even that guy who gave a concert in Falmington last Sunday, what was his name now, Shane Hammond. All these rock stars shine with an aura of sexuality. I'll bet that none of them ever sleep alone except by choice!'

Rosie nodded her head and said: 'I'm sure you're right, but you're not going to sleep alone tonight either, Bruce Teplin. It's a rule of the house that I don't fuck with wham-bam, thank-you ma'am chaps. Don't you lodge with the senior languages tutor Grahame Johnstone at Mrs Highgate's bed and brekkie in Standlake Street? Look, I'm setting the alarm for seven fifteen which will give you ample time to take a nice early morning stroll back to your digs. It shouldn't take you more than twenty minutes and a good walk will give your legs some good exercise.'

Bruce grunted and rolled over to face the gorgeous girl and, planting a kiss on the tip of her nose, he murmured: 'Rosie, I can think of a much better way to exercise my legs.'

She slid her hand down across his belly and grasped his thickening truncheon. 'My word! You can't keep a good cock down,' she said with undisguised admiration as she drew his foreskin down his shaft and then slid the skin back over the swelling knob.

'But you know very well I wasn't talking about your middle leg, you randy so and so!' Rosie went on whilst she continued to masturbate his stiffened organ, and then she gave him a dazzling smile and added: 'On the other hand, there's nothing wrong with working out indoors, is there?'

It would not have bothered Rosie O'Hara if anyone had

seen Bruce Teplin leave her house the next morning. Nevertheless, in case he might be worried about being the subject of gossip, Rosie O'Hara had thought it best not to inform Bruce that two of his students, Marc Ribeaux and Pierre Truchet, were lodging next door or that the two Frenchmen also rarely slept alone.

Both Marc and Pierre were spending the summer brushing up their near-perfect English and studying management economics before leaving for the Harvard Business School in the autumn. The two handsome young Frenchmen had found no shortage of willing bedmates during their stay in the little English seaside town.

However, at the suggestion of Belinda Blisswood, a luscious and extremely horny seventeen-year-old who worked as an assistant receptionist at the Berkeley Hotel, on this particular night they had agreed to share her favours after they had returned home from celebrating Marc's twenty-first birthday at the Cross Keys.

Belinda was slightly surprised when she asked if either of the two youths had taken part in a three-in-a-bed fucking session before. 'I thought you Froggies would be into all naughty games,' said Belinda with a giggle as Marc shamefacedly confessed that this would be a new experience for him.

'But I'm sure I'll enjoy it,' he added as the blonde temptress rubbed her palm down to his groin. His swelling shaft was already tenting his trousers, for Belinda had already stayed the night in their flat in Pierre's bedroom and his friend had already informed him – for to improve their command of colloquial English they never spoke French even to each other – that 'as the Americans put it, she fucks like a rattlesnake!'

Therefore his heart began to pound with excitement when Belinda clasped his hand and cooed: 'Let's go into the bedroom, birthday boy. We'll get warmed up whilst

Pierre tidies up the kitchen. I hate looking at a pile of washing-up before sitting down to breakfast, don't you?'

Marc glanced round to his friend and Pierre winked back as he gave an encouraging grin and then hauled himself out of his chair and said as he left the room: 'Point taken, Belinda, and afterwards I'll hoover the lounge. It looks like a rubbish tip.'

'Don't work too hard, though, I don't want you falling asleep when you come to bed,' she warned as she pulled Marc towards the bedroom where she kissed Marc's ear and whispered: 'I must pop into the bathroom first – don't go away, I'll be back in five minutes.'

'Oh, I'm staying put,' he replied as he sat down on the bed and bent down to untie his shoelaces. He pulled off his shoes, unknotted his tie which he threw over a nearby chair and lay back with his head resting against the pillow. Belinda was as good as her word and soon rejoined him, but when she slid next to him on the bed, Marc noticed that she had removed her bra. He drew in his breath sharply as his eyes swivelled down to Belinda's nubile young breasts which he could see were now bare underneath her transparent silk blouse.

She lay next to him, pressing her soft curves against his lean, muscular frame as she lifted up her pretty face to be kissed. Their mouths met and she swallowed his tongue like a hungry animal whilst her own tongue shot between Marc's lips to slide wetly against his teeth. When he roughly pulled out Belinda's blouse from out of her skirt, she eagerly helped him slip the wispy garment off her shoulders.

Marc pulled his face away for a moment to stare at the girl's succulent bosoms before he cupped the deliciously soft high-tipped globes in his hands. His arms trembled as he felt the hardening nipples push against his fingertips. 'Oh yes, Marc,' she whispered throatily. 'Squeeze my tits.

Squeeze them hard! God, I love it!'

There was now a mountainous swelling in his jeans and Belinda swiftly wrenched off his belt, unzipped his flies and then assisted Marc to wriggle the denims down to his feet. Then Belinda passed her tongue sensuously over her upper lips and she purred contentedly as she tugged Marc's Y-fronts over his hips and freed his thick, pulsing prick which sprung up to salute her.

'My word, you are a big boy,' she murmured as she held his swollen shaft tightly in her hand, making his rigid rod twitch as she slowly worked her fist up and down the fleshy warm truncheon.

'Let's see if you taste as nice as your friend Pierre,' she added as she slithered across him and opening her mouth, swirled her tongue all over the smooth uncapped bulb before sliding her lips over the juicy ripe plum of his glans. Marc let out a low cry of delight as Belinda moved her head slowly downwards and sucked in almost half of his palpitating boner down her throat. She wrapped the fingers of her right hand around the root of his shaft and began to frig him gently whilst her left hand cradled his hairy scrotum, gently caressing his balls, rolling them back and forth as they tightened within their wrinkled pink sack. Above her bobbing head she could hear Marc groan in ecstatic delight when she began her special technique of sucking underneath the rim of his knob, pressing her soft lips wetly against his fleshy column.

Belinda began to swallow in anticipation as Marc's penis started to jerk wildly inside her mouth. When the stream of creamy jism gushed out of his cock she gulped down his sticky emission with genuine enjoyment. He bucked his hips as she sucked his shuddering shaft with great skill, coaxing out the last dribbles of spunk until she had milked him dry. She released his deflated shaft and smacked her lips with evident satisfaction as she lifted her head and said rather unnecessarily: 'There, was that a nice present or would you have preferred a birthday card from W H Smith's instead?'

Marc had time only to gurgle a reply before she pulled her legs across and proceeded to straddle him, moving upwards to sit upon his chest until her damp muff of pussy hair was pressed so tightly against his nostrils that it tickled his nose and made him sneeze.

'Marc Ribeaux, you naughty man,' she scolded him in mock reproof. 'I'm surprised at you. Don't you know that it is considered very rude in England to sneeze into a lady's cunt?'

'My apologies, *cherie*, let me kiss it better,' he muttered and then he raked his tongue along the length of Belinda's moist crack.

'Your apology is accepted,' she replied with a gasp as she adjusted her position to open herself even further for his questing tongue. Marc slurped lustily as he drew her pouting pussy lips into his mouth, lapping up the aromatic love juice which was now trickling freely from her love channel. Her hips drew up with added urgency as he found her erect clitty which had burst out from between her love lips and he started to attack the fleshy nub with a series of quick little nips.

She clutched at his head and began to pant violently as Marc continued to flick his tongue in and out of her juicy cunt at an ever-increasing speed. Both were so engrossed in this passionate exercise that neither of them heard Pierre enter the room, holding an opened bottle of baby lotion in his hand. He was stark naked and his circumcised cock, which was already semi-erect, swelled up to its fullest height when he smeared a liberal amount of lotion onto his shaft.

Pierre climbed up on the bed and carefully parted Marc's legs to give himself room to kneel behind Belinda.

He placed his hands on her shapely arse and slowly pulled them slightly apart as he savoured the dimpled contours of her outspread rear. When Belinda felt his cool hands on her backside she slid her arm around Marc's neck and kept his face pressed against her cunt. She wriggled her body backwards, shifting her firm buttocks back towards Pierre's belly as he slipped his cock into the crevice between her bum cheeks.

'Hold it steady, I'll get it in,' she panted and Pierre obediently held his throbbing shaft still whilst Belinda rubbed the broad top of his helmet into her bottom, deliberately relaxing the muscles as she pushed her body backwards against him.

'*Mon Dieu!*' grunted Pierre and he watched with growing excitement as she deftly introduced his broad knob inside the starfish-shaped ring of her anus. Then suddenly he found his cock jammed inside the narrow sheath and he gasped as the tight warmth enveloped him whilst Marc gulped down the gush of cuntal juice which flowed out of Belinda's pussy as she responded to the force of Pierre's prick penetrating her back passage.

He continued to lick out her sopping cunny whilst Pierre's well-greased tool pistoned in and out of her bum. She shrieked with delight as ripples of utter bliss flowed out from her crotch and Marc swallowed as much as he could of the rivulet of tangy love juice which flowed out from her sated cunt as Pierre slid forward one final time and creamed her arsehole with a fountain of sticky spunk.

Belinda and Pierre collapsed into a heap, squashing Marc's face underneath the girl's dripping cunt until he was able to extricate his nose and mouth from the wet prison of her pussy.

For some strange reason, a vaguely remembered phrase from her school history book came to Belinda's mind and she asked blithely: 'So tell me, my two French friends, would you say that the three of us strengthened the *Entente Cordiale* tonight?'

'Oh yes, without doubt,' murmured Pierre as his fingers closed over one of her still perky nipples. 'If the rest of your countrymen were as keen on joining Europe, President de Gaulle wouldn't be able to keep Britain out of the Common Market.'

'Oh that,' she sighed as she slicked her hand lazily up and down Marc's burgeoning shaft. 'I've never understood all this Common Market business. Does that mean that if we join, we can't have a Queen any more and everyone on the Continent has to speak English or is it the other way round?'

Marc raised his eyes to the ceiling and remarked: 'I don't think there's much danger of anything like that, Belinda, but in any case I often wonder whether Britain will ever become part of Europe.'

'But we are already,' objected Belinda as she skinned his hood and bent down to wiggle the point of her tongue under the rim of his swollen bellend. 'Didn't Britain win the Eurovision Song Contest this year? You know, Sandie Shaw, the girl who doesn't wear any shoes, sang *Puppet On A String*. Now how did it go, oh yes——'

'This is quite true,' said Pierre hastily, covering Belinda's lips with a smacking wet kiss before she could draw breath. 'But now that Marc has had his birthday present for which I know he is very grateful, I'm afraid it is time to break up the party. It's well after midnight and Marc and I still have some preparation for the seminar we have tomorrow with our tutor Dr Teplin. He's never late so we won't have any time to finish our work if we don't get up early. In any case, you said you're on the eight o'clock shift tomorrow morning so we had all better get dressed and I'll take you home on my scooter.'

Belinda nodded and, with her hand still clasped around

Marc's swollen shaft and her tongue swirling around his knob, she looked at her watch and sighed: 'Yes, I suppose you're right, Pierre. Wait a moment though, I can't leave poor Marc like this. It won't take a minute for me to finish him off.'

Pierre grinned and his own beefy tool began to thicken as he watched. The girl held Marc's prick tightly at the base with her left hand whilst she clasped the fingers of her right hand around the veiny shaft and pumped her fist up and down in long, slow pulling strokes. Sure enough, in under thirty seconds his cock began to twitch with the lurching spasms which heralded the arrival of a fully-blown climax.

'Ohhh!' gasped Marc as he ejaculated and a spurting arc of spunk squirted out of his cock to land on Belinda's fingers and a following stream of sticky seed flowed out from the tiny 'eye' on the top of his helmet.

'Sorry it had to be so quick,' she apologised as she licked off his creamy jism from her fingers before sitting up and sliding her legs into her knickers. 'Happy birthday again, Marc, we'll have another threesome soon if you fancy.'

'Oh yes, I fancy,' said Marc, mopping his brow as his head fell back onto his pillows.

Although Rosie O'Hara did not accompany him on the short walk from her apartment to the College – her first lecture was not until mid-day and she preferred to mark her students' papers in the quiet of her own home – Bruce Teplin was still concerned that someone might see him leave her flat and start a chain of gossip which was likely to reach the ears of his girl friend who was visiting him in a fortnight's time.

'No, you never know,' he muttered to himself, bliss-fully unaware that as he hurried away from Rosie's front door, Marc Ribeaux happened to be staring out of the window whilst he munched on a piece of toast. The Frenchman saw the tall figure of the lecturer close the front door behind him and then walk briskly across the road where he boarded a red single-decker bus which had just drawn up to take him back to his lodgings.

The bus roared away and Marc let out a hoarse chuckle and called out to his flatmate: 'Hey, Pierre, you will never believe who I have just seen coming out of Rosie O'Hara's house.'

'Wait a moment, don't tell me,' said Pierre as he ambled across to the window. 'Nick Armitage, perhaps or Steven Williams? On the other hand, it could be any of our friends because every bloody student in Falmington College wants to fuck her!'

'That's true enough, but it wasn't a student,' said Marc with a grin. 'The lucky man was none other than our beloved tutor, Dr Bruce Teplin.'

'Dr Bruce Teplin? Are you quite sure?' Pierre queried disbelievingly. 'How very surprising, I wouldn't have thought he did anything in bed except read *The Economist* or *Financial Times*.'

'Oh, I'm certain it was him. He didn't turn left to walk up to the College but ran across the road to catch a bus back to town, probably to get home and pick up whatever he needs for the seminar.'

'The lucky man, I envy him,' Pierre grunted as he sat down at the desk to check out some notes he had made at Bruce Teplin's last lecture. 'Well, at least he should be in a good mood and won't be too critical of any mistakes we might make if he calls on us to speak this morning.'

'Let's hope you're right,' said Marc as he looked away from the window and said: 'Look, I think I'll go now to the College and read through that chapter on inflation in MacGregor's *Applied Economics* that Brucie is bound to question us about. Do you want to come with me or will you come in later?'

'I'll come later,' answered Pierre as he selected one of the books which were piled up in front of him. 'I can study easier here. In the library there are too many girls walking around in mini-skirts for me to concentrate properly. Let's meet up at a quarter to ten outside Dr Teplin's office. I have to return a book to him and then we can compare our notes before going in to the seminar.'

'Okay, see you there,' said Marc. After finishing his breakfast he packed his case and left the flat five minutes later. He enjoyed the short walk to the College in the bright August sunshine and was gravely tempted to buy a newspaper and sit out on one of the benches in the nearby public gardens for ten minutes. However, he needed a good mark at the end of his course – preferably with a commendation from Dr Teplin – and though he wobbled towards expediency when he passed by Mr Patel's corner store, in the end he settled for principle and made his way towards the library.

Once there he sat down and noticed Denise Cochran sitting just two seats away on his left. He flashed a wide smile towards her as she lifted a book out of her briefcase. She smiled back and for a second time Marc was tempted to leave his studies, this time to move across and chat to the pretty girl whom he had tried without success to chat up after the first week at the College. Denise had been friendly enough but she had tactfully rebuffed his advances and soon afterwards someone told him of Denise's close friendship with Sharon Shaw, Dr Teplin's secretary.

'They are both, how you say, lesbians?' he had said sadly, hardly comforted by the information that it was rumoured that Denise at least swung both ways. 'What a shocking waste, Denise is a most attractive girl and Sharon is terribly sexy. She reminds me of the young Brigitte Bardot.'

So with a sigh he opened his copy of *Applied Economics* by Professor Iain MacGregor. Placing his elbows on the table, he sunk his chin down onto the bridge formed by his entwined fingers and settled down to his studies.

Whilst Marc and Denise concentrated on their books, upstairs in Dr Teplin's office, Sharon Shaw was sitting in the lecturer's chair with an impish smile on her lips. She had sorted out the post and as he had instructed, she had opened all the letters addressed to her boss except for a thick white envelope which unlike the others had Bruce Teplin's name written across it in a bold dark ballpoint scrawl as opposed to a neat typewritten label. Sharon had slit open the envelope and pulled out three sheets of notepaper which had been written on in a neat feminine hand. She saw the words *All my love, Katie* at the foot of the letter and then she turned over the sheaf and chuckled as she read *Darling Brucie*. This was obviously a private love letter from Bruce Teplin's girl friend – but why hadn't she posted it to his private address instead of to the College?

Well, there's only one way to find out and Dr Teplin did tell me to open all his mail, muttered Sharon to herself as she unfolded the sheets of paper and with growing interest read the following letter:

Darling Brucie,

Thanks for your lovely letter which I received last Tuesday. I'm sorry you're finding life dull down in Falmington, but think of that nice fat cheque you're going to get next month! Then we'll fly down to Sorrento and stay at that posh hotel which your head of studies at the L.S.E. recommended to you. Just imagine how wonderful it will be to sunbathe all day, boogie till the small hours and then fuck like crazy for the rest of the night! Oooh, the very thought of it is making me horny!

In the meantime I've been having a pretty quiet time in Swinging London without you. I've been catching up on my reading, tidying the flat, and staying in most nights although last Sunday Jill Anthony dragged me out to the pictures to see The Trip. It's a new psychedelic film with Peter Fonda, all about a director of TV commercials who has these weird hallucinations after taking LSD. Some good effects but someone like you who likes a strong storyline wouldn't like it as it's a pretty plotless film.

But the big event of the week, and the most exciting thing that's happened to me since you went to Falmington, took place yesterday morning at work. You know that I left Guys Hospital to work in Harley Street not only because I was fed-up with shift work but because I knew that Doctor Yenta treated a lot of show business personalities and I thought it might be a lot of fun meeting them.

Well, talk about coincidence, you'll never guess who came to see Doctor Yenta – and this is STRICTLY CONFIDENTIAL because I shouldn't even mention patients' names to anyone not connected with their medical treatment – but when the receptionist called me on the phone and told me that Mr Shane Hammond had arrived for his appointment and was sitting in the waiting-room, I don't mind admitting that I went weak at the knees at the thought of meeting one of the most famous rock stars in the world.

All right, Brucie, you old square, I know that you prefer Beethoven to the Beatles and Ravel to the Rolling Stones. But Shane isn't just one of these *here-today-gone-tomorrow pop stars – otherwise you would have been able to get tickets for us to see him at that concert he gave in Falmington the other week* – and of course off-stage he's almost as well-known as being a tremendous stag and shagging God only knows how many teenage groupies as well as having an affair with Diana Windsor, the sexy girl with long red hair who plays the young schoolmistress in that TV soap opera* Copperwood Park, *the show you say you never watch and yet you always ask me what's been happening if you miss an episode!*

Anyhow, I peeped into the waiting room and saw that Shane Hammond was dressed in a denim jacket with fringes on the sleeves and the tightest pair of jeans I'd ever seen. I couldn't help dropping my eyes to look at the bulge of his cock and balls as he stood up when I went in to bring him upstairs to the consulting rooms. He was very quiet in the lift but when I told him how much I enjoyed his music, he gave me a lovely little smile and murmured: 'Thank you, I'm so glad,' as I opened the door and announced his arrival to Doctor Yenta.

Now then, Brucie, I have a confession to make, and it's just the first so don't be too shocked about it. As Shane shook hands with the doctor, I went through into my room, but instead of shutting the door firmly behind me as I should have done, I deliberately kept it slightly ajar and, by positioning myself next to the filing cabinet with some papers in my hand, I had an excuse to be standing where I could see Shane and hear everything that the two of them were saying.

I could tell from the way he was wriggling about on

---

* See 'Summer School 2: All Night Girls' [New English Library]

his chair that Shane was embarrassed when Doctor Yenta asked him just what was the problem which was bothering him, he replied: 'Well, the fact of the matter, Doc, is that I've been feeling very tired lately. True, I've been working very hard. The band only finished a seven-city, three-week tour on Tuesday, we've a concert at the Albert Hall on Saturday night and next week we're scheduled to go into the studios at Abbey Road and make a new LP, even though I still haven't finished writing one of the songs I promised to have ready for the new record.'

'For heaven's sake, Shane, it's no wonder you're feeling tired,' commented my employer. Dr Jonathan Yenta is one of the top urologists in the country and it was not that difficult to guess why Shane had come to see him, so I was not entirely surprised when Shane said: 'Yeah, that's all very well but I've been much more tired and still managed to bounce back. When we first made it we packed up our own gear and copped a quick kip in the back of the van before getting home and going to work.

'Then we started making a bit of a name for ourselves and we got even less sleep when the groupies came round after the show – but now it wouldn't be worth it for them because I couldn't give them a special performance, if you get my drift.'

'Oh, I think I do,' remarked Doctor Yenta with a smile. 'To put it bluntly, what you're telling me is that you're having a problem getting it up and even if you do get a hard-on you're coming too quickly.'

'You've got it in one, Doc,' said Shane with a sigh. 'And before you ask me any questions, take no notice of what you read in the papers. My publicity guy might feed them stories about Wild Shane Hammond, but I'm not a great boozer, I don't smoke and the only drug I take is a paracetamol tablet now and then when I have a headache.'

Doctor Yenta looked at him over the top of his glasses and said: 'I believe you, Mr Hammond, I believe you, and certainly alcohol and drugs are often the causes of sexual dysfunction. But there are several psychological reasons as well, you know. To be frank with you, as far as many of my show business patients are concerned, one of the most common explanations for this kind of problem is their feeling of guilt in having a quick knee-trembler with a chorus girl or groupie and then worrying that they might have passed on an infection to their partners.'

Shane did not take up the bait and sat silently whilst Doctor Yenta rose from his chair and continued: 'Still, let me give you a thorough examination and we'll see if there's anything physically wrong with you. I doubt it very much but at least it will put your mind at rest.'

At this stage I closed the door but ten minutes later Doctor Yenta came in and said: 'Nurse, I need some specimens from Mr Hammond. I've sent him upstairs to one of the cubicles, would you please collect them for me please and then take them over to the laboratory?'

'Of course, Doctor Yenta,' I said as I climbed the stairs I must admit that I was beginning to feel horny at the thought that I might get a chance to take a quick peek at Shane Hammond's prick. My panties were getting damp when I remembered that tasty looking bulge in his jeans and wondered how well-hung he might be and I was fantasising about him tossing off his big cock when I knocked on the door.

'Come in,' he called out and when I opened the door, there was the one and only showbiz stud sitting *on a hard chair with his underpants and jeans around his feet. Although he was covering himself with his hands I could just see the knob of his beefy semi-erect chopper peeping out from between his fingers.*

'Hi there,' he said gloomily. 'My water specimen is in the jar on the floor and the test tube for the other one is on the floor next to me but I'm having some trouble with this other sample Doctor Yenta has asked me to provide. I'm worried enough about problems with my equipment and this cubicle isn't exactly the sexiest location I've ever been in.'

I closed the door behind me and said: 'Don't fret, Mr Hammond, you're not the first man who's had a similar problem, I promise you. We try to keep a copy of Knave *in here but it's always being taken away, usually by Arab or Japanese patients who can't buy girlie magazines at home.*

'Let me see if I can give you a helping hand,' I added softly as I unfastened the front of my white tunic and sank down on my knees so that he could see my breasts squeezed together in my tight half-cup bra. I placed his hands on my boobs and said encouragingly: 'Why don't you lift them out? One look at my tits should do the trick.'

'Thank you, Nurse,' he said and Shane's eyes glinted as he slid his palms under my bosoms and slipped them out into his hands whilst I swung my hands behind me to unhook the catch of my bra. I looked across at his shaft which was now almost fully erect and I wrapped my fingers round it and began to wank him, not too quickly and soon his thick prick was standing as stiff as could be. It was a good size, about eight inches long, and I really enjoyed swirling my tongue around the uncapped helmet which made him shudder and I lifted my head and said: 'Give me

the test-tube, Shane, it won't take long now to get the sample Doctor Yenta wants from you.'

He bent down and passed it over to me as I started to fist my hand quickly up and down his blue-veined stiffie. 'Oh God, I'm coming,' he moaned and with my free hand I slipped the top of the plastic tube over his bell-end whilst I continued to wank him. A few seconds later his spunk splashed out into the tube and by the time I had finished milking his twitching tool Doctor Yenta had enough semen for twenty tests let alone the half dozen or so which were carried out in the laboratory.

'There, that wasn't so bad, was it?' I said cheerfully and he stammered: 'No, it was great, thank you very much. I've always enjoyed being tossed off, but my cock hasn't been as hard as that for over a week.'

'Well, it only goes to show that it's hardly worthwhile even sending your samples to the lab,' I observed whilst I unzipped my skirt and watched his eyes widen as I let it fall to the floor and stood before him dressed only in a pair of tiny white panties which were already very moist!

I moved closer to him and pulled his head against my thighs and whispered: 'Lick my pussy, Shane, ream out my quim, there's a good boy!' and then it was my turn to groan when I felt his tongue brushing against the wet crotch of my knickers. My whole body began to shudder when he rolled them down to the ground and buried his face in my furry bush. I yelped with delight when he stuck his head between my legs and planted a series of wet little kisses on my cunny lips.

Then I moved one foot up on the chair and I came almost immediately after he slid his tongue into my love funnel. Shane smacked his lips as he gulped *down the cunt juice which was pulsing out of my pussy in little love-spurts whilst I ground my hairy mound against his face. He soon found my clitty with his probing tongue and he sucked me up really marvellously to a shattering climax. By the time he stopped to catch his breath, his shaft was standing up to attention again, if anything looking even stiffer and harder than before.*

I grabbed hold of his hot cock and gave it a swift wank as I said: 'How about producing another sample, Shane? This time, though, we'll use my quim rather than a test-tube.'

'Then I turned round and bent over and stuck out my backside, giving it a little wiggle as Shane smoothed his hands across my bum cheeks and I thrilled with pleasure when I felt his rampant truncheon rest under the crease of my buttocks.

He kissed the back of my neck and I wiggled my bottom again against his cock, feeling it sliding between my thighs. 'Put it in,' I panted, trembling with anticipation as he slid his hand round across my thigh to open up my cunt with his fingers. I pressed my hands against the wall and squirmed with pleasure as his fingertips gently kneaded the soft folds of my pussy whilst he glided the thick crown of his cock along the cleft between my bum cheeks towards my yearning quim.

I braced myself against his plunging entry and gasped as he firmly embedded his rock hard rammer inside me until his belly was slap up against my bottom. Then he pulled back and began to fuck me with quick short strokes alternating with slower deeper ones. It was wonderful! I felt my knees buckle as he slewed his shaft in and out of my juicy love-box and as soon as he drenched my cunt with his jism, my pussy exploded and I yelled out in triumph as he fucked me to a sizzling gut-wrenching orgasm.

When we had recovered I told him to get dressed as quickly as possible in case Doctor Yenta came looking for us and I said to him shamelessly: 'Well, Shane, now I'm even more sure that the laboratory boys will find nothing wrong with your wedding tackle. But if you want to come back and give us another sample, I'll be waiting for you.'

Of course he didn't need to come back because Doctor Yenta called him the very next day to tell him that all the tests were negative. Last Friday Shane himself called to say that all was now well and he was again enjoying his usual hectic sex life. Though I still don't know what caused Shane's temporary problems between the sheets, the odds are it was sheer tiredness due to overwork coupled with the fact that he was frightened that Diana Windsor might find out that he had screwed two of the dancers last month after he topped the bill on the Sunday Night At The London Palladium *show.*

So there we are, Bruce, I've been a very bad girl and you'll have to give my bum a good smacking when I get down to Falmington next week – but you won't mind doing that too much, will you?

Not that I feel guilty about being shagged by Shane Hammond because I'm certain that you've been up to some rumpy-pumpy with one of those girls you were telling me about on your course. Or are you having it away with that luscious young secretary you've been telling me about. Never mind those rumours about her being a lezzie, there's only one way to find out if she's interested in men and that's to ask her! Fair heart never won fair lady and all that jazz!

Looking forward to seeing you soon. I might be able to come down next weekend.

All my love
Katie

Sharon whistled softly as she folded the sheets of note-paper and fastened them together with a paper-clip before putting them on top of the pile of post in Bruce Teplin's in-tray. Then she glanced up at the clock on the wall and raised her eyebrows when she saw that it was almost twenty-five past nine, at least ten minutes after the time her normally ultra-punctual boss arrived for work. He's probably still in bed, pulling his pud whilst thinking about Katie, Sharon decided uncharitably as she picked up a memo addressed to her which Bruce Teplin had written after she had left work the previous evening. However, this note was in a very different vein and simply read:

Sharon, in case you have not arrived by the time I leave to take my seminar tomorrow morning, would you please contact Sir Stafford Stiffkey, the Member of Parliament for Falmington, who on my behalf has kindly collected some important documents on governmental intervention in macro-economic affairs during the late nineteen-fifties from various sources in Whitehall. If possible, would you go round to his house before lunch and pick up these papers as I would like to begin work on them this afternoon. His telephone number is Falmington 9851 and he lives at Austin Manor, Coppice Walk, West Falmington. If necessary, sign an I.O.U. for the taxi fare and I will sign an expenses chit when you return. He is expecting a call tomorrow morning and I suggest you telephone him between nine thirty and ten o'clock.

> *Incidentally, Sir Stafford is the guest of honour and will present the diplomas awarded to summer school students at the College's Annual Open Day on September 2nd.*

Macro-economic affairs, Sharon muttered as she checked through the rest of the papers in the in-tray, what the heck are they about when they're at home? I bet they're not as interesting as the kind of affairs some MPs get up to after those late-night sittings. Still, it would be nice to get out of the office on such a nice summery day and with a bit of luck she could spin out the job to take up most of the morning.

But what was keeping Bruce Teplin, she wondered as she looked up again at the hands of his clock which were now approaching half past nine.

As she had promised, Rosie O'Hara had set her bedside alarm clock for seven fifteen. But she had forgotten to rewind it and it was already eight o'clock when her eyes fluttered open. She rolled herself out from under Bruce Teplin's arm which was thrown across her body and let out an irritated moan when she looked at the clock and saw that she and Bruce had overslept. She was in no rush to get up – her only lecture that day was in the afternoon – but she felt duty-bound to wake Bruce who was still fast asleep, breathing heavily with a small smile playing about his lips.

Rosie rolled back to face him and felt his stiff cock press against her belly. 'No prize for guessing what you've been dreaming about,' she said softly as she smoothed her hand across Bruce's cheek and moved her body across him to whisper in his ear: 'Wake up, lover, or you'll be late for your seminar.'

To her astonishment, Bruce Teplin grunted and swung

his arms around her sensuous curves. 'Fuck the seminar!' he growled throatily and Rosie's eyes twinkled with delight. She was gratified to discover more evidence that the economist was far from being the mere 'desiccated calculating machine' another female member of the teaching staff had called Bruce Teplin after making his acquaintance at a staff cocktail party.

'By all means, but I'd much rather you fucked me first,' she chuckled as she eagerly grasped his erect penis and rubbed the rock-hard tool until it began to pulse and twitch between her fingers.

'A-a-a-h! A-a-a-h! A-a-a-h!' he breathed roughly through his mouth as Rosie lowered her head and washed his knob with her wet tongue and he groaned as she licked sensuously around the ridge of his helmet. Then she lifted up her face to allow Bruce to pull her head towards him. Their bodies pressed together as he forced open her lips and plunged his tongue into her mouth, squashing his swollen shaft between their bellies as they rolled from side to side. Their lips were crushed together as their hands and fingers patted and petted, caressed and stroked as great shivers of erotic desire rocked through their bodies.

Then Bruce clambered up and knelt between her thighs, holding his bursting erection in one hand as he slid one of his pillows underneath her bottom with the other. Rosie lay back and thrust her hips forward as she placed her long legs over his shoulders.

He nudged the tip of his bared purple bell-end into the folds of her pussy, rubbing it against her cunny lips to stimulate the flow of love juice which was already moistening Rosie's cunt, ready to welcome Bruce's hot stiff cock at its desired destination.

'Stick it in me, Brucie, I want your cock inside my cunny,' she groaned, bracing herself for the coming onslaught. A warm, satisfying glow spread through the trembling girl as he eased his fleshy truncheon into the full length of her creamy cunt. Bruce shivered with pleasure as his cock slid firmly into place and Rosie's tight tunnel sucked it in and closed around his throbbing tool.

Bruce let out a low sigh as he sank into her wet warmth. The clinging muscles of her quim gently massaged his pulsating penis with a sensuous snake-like motion. For a moment or two he lay still, delighting in the thrill of the intimate sensations, and then he began to fuck her, pistoning his prick to and fro in short, jabbing strokes.

'Deeper, darling, deeper! I want to feel every inch of your lovely big cock in my cunt!' she called out wildly. She clasped her feet together around the back of his neck as he obediently buried his chopper into her juicy quim until their pubic hairs mashed together.

'There we go!' he gasped as he furiously rammed his rigid rod in and out of her hungry hole. They both could hear the erotic squelching noise made by their lustful love-making as Bruce's cock slewed in and out of her dripping honeypot broken by the rhythmic slip-slap sound made by his ballsack bouncing against her bottom.

He bore down on her again, his lean frame soaked with sweat as he fucked her in a mad fever of passion, sending electric shocks of the sweetest pleasure crackling out of her crotch whilst the rippling movement of his thick shaft made her body buck and twist in sheer bliss.

'Come with me, lover, I'm there, over the top we go!' cried out Rosie and the pair melted into a magnificent mutual orgasm, coming together as, with one final lunge, Bruce shot a tremendous stream of spunk into her sopping sheath. He felt Rosie shudder beneath him as she reached her climax and her cunt gushed a final fierce spurt of love juice as their bodies slithered against each other as they writhed in the passionate throes of ecstasy until, sated by their frenzied pleasure, they slumped down in an erotic tangle of naked limbs.

'Phew, if there's a better way to start the day, I'd like to know what it is,' remarked Rosie thoughtfully as she snuggled into the crook of his shoulder. 'Wouldn't it be nice to stay in bed all morning? Oh Bruce, I hate to mention it but it's almost a quarter past eight. You'd better get up and get dressed if you're going to go back home before setting off for your seminar.'

'Blow the seminar! I'd much rather stay here with you,' replied the lecturer, pulling a pillow over his head. But Rosie pulled it off him and said firmly: 'Well, I'd rather you stayed here as well but you must go, Brucie. It's not fair on the students and anyhow, you would feel guilty afterwards and then blame me.

'So up we get,' she added cheerfully as she threw off the eiderdown and hauled herself off the sheets. 'Time for a quick coffee before you hit the road?'

Ten minutes later Bruce Teplin opened the front door and walked briskly across the road to catch a bus back to his lodgings, blissfully unaware that he was being watched by Marc Ribeaux.

In the College library Denise Cochran opened her handbag and brought out the letter which the postman had thrust into her hand an hour or so ago outside her apartment just as she and Sharon were leaving home. She looked at the Bloomsbury postmark on the envelope and correctly guessed that the sender was George Radlett, the editorial director of Chelmsford and Parrish. This could be interesting, she thought, as she slit open the envelope with her index finger, took out the letter and read:

Dear Denise,
    Here's some exciting news from company HQ –

I've heard it on the grapevine that Shane Hammond, the rock star, is putting the finishing touches to his autobiography and how his band, the Hurricanes, came to be formed. No-one has yet been given sight of the script but the word is that Shane lifts the lid on some of the murkier practices of the music business and this alone is bound to make the book a huge bestseller. Shane goes on his first US tour this Autumn so whoever buys the world rights could flog the book for a fortune to the Yanks, let alone what could be made from a newspaper serialisation in this country and the French and German rights.

Well, I need hardly tell you that our only chance of snapping up a book like this is to get ahead of the big boys who can offer far bigger advances than us. But I understand that Shane's manager, Mr Lennie Lieberman, hasn't yet contacted any literary agents so we have a chance to make a pre-emptive bid if we can get through to Shane and convince him (and Mr Lieberman who'll probably be quite a tough nut to crack) that everyone at Chelmsford and Parrish will put their heart and soul into publishing his masterpiece.

Now this is where you come in, Denise. My source (a miniskirted dollybird in Lennie Lieberman's office who happens to be a close friend of my younger brother, the lucky beggar) has told us that she has booked a room for Shane at the Berkeley Hotel, Falmington-On-Sea this coming weekend. It seems he was smitten by a girl named Sandie he met at a concert he gave in Falmington a couple of weeks ago – he's booked in under a pseudonym, of course, he'll arrive wearing a false beard or in some other disguise and register as Mr Michael Reynolds.

So what would be wonderful is if you could wangle a way to meet the great man and fill his ear about how

*we would publish his book far better than anyone
else! Carys Thomas tells me that you wrote to her
saying how much you enjoyed Shane's concert so you
could talk to him about his music far more knowledg-
ably than anyone else here.*

*Perhaps you could even gauge the kind of advance
he's looking for. If he wants a hard and fast offer call
me immediately and I'll be down on the next train –
you have my home telephone number if you need to
reach me out of office hours.*

*Of course, this could well come to nothing, but it
must be worth a try. Don't hesitate to contact me if
there's any further information I can give you. Obviously, this business must be kept under your hat,
don't breathe a word to anybody. If you speak to
someone in the office, don't even mention this project
to anyone else. In fact, I'd be happier if you tore up
this letter into little pieces after you've read it!*

Best of luck,
George

Denise drew her hand slowly across her cheek whilst she
considered the gist of George Radlett's idea. It certainly
would be a feather in their caps if they could pull off this
coup, but she was sensible enough to realise that there
was only a slight chance of scooping the other publishers
with a pre-emptive strike. She was inclined to agree with
George's comment that it was unlikely they would suc-
ceed – but nothing ventured, nothing gained as her
Grandma always used to tell her.

In any case, it would be great fun to meet Shane
Hammond and she suddenly remembered that one of
Sharon's friends worked as a receptionist at the Berkeley
Hotel. What was her name now? she frowned and then

her brow cleared as she remembered the girl's name. A stunning seventeen-year-old like Belinda Blisswood might provide just the *entrée* into Shane Hammond's suite that she needed . . .

She smiled as she slid George's letter into her file and she decided to see if she could have a quick word with Sharon before the seminar. She gathered her books and papers together and made her way to Bruce Teplin's office where she found a gaggle of fellow students waiting outside his door including Marc and Pierre, the two French boys with whom she was particularly friendly.

'Hi there, guys, what's going on here? Where's our beloved leader?' she asked but Marc shrugged his shoulders and replied: 'No-one knows, so we thought we would wait in his office. Sharon doesn't know where he has got to either so she's ringing his boarding house to see if he's still there and then she'll tell us if she's had any success in finding him.'

He chuckled as he leaned forward and added in a low voice: 'Between ourselves, I think Dr Teplin might be too tired to take his seminar this morning. I happened to see him leaving Rosie O'Hara's flat at half past eight this morning.'

'Did you really? I wouldn't have thought he was her type,' remarked Denise in some surprise. 'On the other hand he could have just gone in to give her a book or something before coming here. He could be caught up in a meeting with the Principal, you know.'

'No, we've checked with Dr Radleigh's office, he's not there,' he replied, shaking his head. 'I will bet you a shortbread biscuit and a cup of coffee that Sharon will come back and say Dr Teplin is unwell and that we can have the morning off.'

'Here's hoping,' said Denise as Sharon came bustling

up to them. 'Well, did you discover where Dr Teplin's got to?'

'Yes, I had a quick word with him,' she replied and she called out: 'Listen, please everybody. Dr Teplin's feeling under the weather and the seminar is postponed till tomorrow morning, same time, same place.'

This announcement hardly displeased the students who could now decide whether they should spend the morning sunbathing in the College grounds or on the beach. The crowd soon dispersed leaving only Denise, Sharon and the two French boys outside Dr Teplin's office.

'I'll have my coffee after lunch,' asked Marc and Denise punched him lightly on the arm and protested: 'I never accepted the bet, you rotter. Anyhow, you should be inviting me out somewhere, I'm still waiting to see some of that smooth gallic charm that's supposed to bring the girls flocking to you like bees to a honeypot.'

'Flocking?' questioned Pierre with a frown. '*Que'est ce que ce* flocking? Is this another word for fucking?'

'Not really, *mon brave*, although in your case it probably is,' promptly answered Denise as she winked at Sharon and went on: 'I have some work to catch up on but how about going down to the beach at lunchtime?'

'What a good idea,' enthused Marc and he turned to Sharon and said: 'You'll come too, I hope, and please bring this yellow bikini which you told us your sister sent you from Carnaby Street last week. I will bring my new Super-8 movie camera and we'll have some fun.'

'Sure, that sounds great,' agreed Sharon enthusiastically. 'Let's meet up at half past twelve in my office. Denise and I will have to stop off at our flat to pick up our cozzies and some towels.'

'Fine, we'll see you then,' said Marc and the two Frenchmen went off back to the library. Sharon was also about to move away when Denise pulled her back by her arm. 'Darling, can we pop across to the canteen for a coffee. You can't have all that much work to do and I want to talk to you about a letter I received from my boss this morning.'

Sharon glanced at her watch. 'Okay, but I can't be too long. I have to pick up some stuff for Bruce this morning and I've booked a taxi to pick me up at half-past ten.' She followed Denise down the corridor and through to the college refectory where, over a cup of coffee, Denise made Sharon pledge her word of honour that she would not reveal details of what she was about to tell her.

'Crikey, what's this all about? Are you now going to tell me that Denise Cochran is only an alias and that really you're an MI5 agent on the track of a master Soviet spy who's been operating out of the College? Who can it be? Bruce Teplin? Rosie O'Hara? Or is it the Principal, the one and only Dr Edwin Radleigh?'

Denise grinned and lightly smacked her friend's hand. 'Don't be daft,' she replied. 'You've been watching too many James Bond films, that's your trouble. Look, be serious a minute and just read this letter from my boss.'

'My God, Shane Hammond's coming back to Falmington!' exclaimed Sharon and Denise placed a finger on her lips as she looked round to make sure that no-one had heard her. 'Hush now, remember, we mustn't let anyone know otherwise I won't have a chance to sign him up for a book.'

'But what an amazing coincidence this is. I've been reading about Shane only this morning,' said Sharon excitedly and she proceeded to tell Denise about the letter from Bruce Teplin's girl friend about how she helped Shane to regain his confidence after his problems with his recalcitrant cock.

'That's a great story, I wonder if he's written about it in his autobiography,' mused Denise thoughtfully. 'Could you copy out this girl Katie's address before you give Bruce his letter? It could be useful if we ever get to publish the book.

'Unfortunately though, she can't help us get to Shane this weekend. But isn't your friend Belinda Blisswood a receptionist at the Berkeley Hotel? Couldn't she find out when "Mr Reynolds" is due to arrive and let us know which room he's been allocated?'

'I don't see why not, but we'd better give Belinda a clue as to why we're so keen to find out the details of this guest's visit. She's bound to give him the once-over when he signs in if she's on duty when he turns up,' Sharon remarked with a frown. 'Belinda's a nice girl but she likes to know what's going on. Funnily enough, she's a great Shane Hammond fan. She's bought all his records and has a huge colour poster of him stuck on her bedroom wall. Honestly, I'd be most surprised if she didn't recognise him.'

Denise spread out her hands and said: 'Well, that's a chance we'll have to take. Anyhow, with a bit of luck she might not be on duty when he arrives. Still, you've got a good point. Let's dream up some pretty dull reason why I want to see Mr Reynolds. Um, why don't you simply tell her that this guy is an old flame of mine from my student days who I haven't seen for two years and it would be a nice surprise for us both if I suddenly turned up.'

'Good enough,' Sharon nodded as she picked up her handbag and said: 'I'll try and get hold of Belinda when I get back from Sir Stafford Stiffkey's place with Bruce's papers. Oh, and don't worry, I'll also make sure that she doesn't blab anything to Pierre Truchet. She's been seeing a lot of him since they met at that disco we had here at the beginning of the summer school term.'

'Thanks, love,' said Denise gratefully as she blew her friend a farewell kiss. 'No-one must know about Shane –

George Radlett is so paranoid about me keeping all this stuff under my hat that he asked me to tear up his letter after I've read it. I suppose I'm lucky he didn't tell me to eat it!'

Her blonde young bed-mate laughed as she pulled back her chair. 'See you later,' she said as she stood up. 'And for heaven's sake, stop worrying – my lips are sealed.'

This was more than could be said of Angela Amos, Sir Stafford Stiffkey's secretary who at that very minute was lying naked on her back on the Member of Parliament's bed, fondling herself with a large vibrator which Sir Stafford had brought back for her from his recent visit to Amsterdam with the Anglo-Dutch Parliamentary Group.

The three-day visit had been a great success although it was as well that no journalists from the British press were present to record how all cross-party differences had been forgotten on the Parliamentarians' last night in the city when, with two other Conservatives, one Liberal and two Labour members of the House of Commons, Sir Stafford had visited *Chez Harold*, one of the most notorious of Amsterdam's private sex clubs in the red-light district.

There he had been deliciously sucked off by a gorgeous long-haired Danish dollybird as he busied himself licking out the pungent pussy of a sallow-skinned Indonesian beauty sitting on a stool whilst she masturbated the Liberal MP and then thrust back her bottom off the seat to allow one of his well-known Conservative colleagues from a marginal West Country constituency to slide his stiff nine-inch tool inside the crevice between her chubby bum cheeks and into her wrinkled little arsehole.

'I just adore getting off on a vibrator,' said Angela chattily to Sir Stafford as he sat watching her rub the head of the hand-held sex toy around the soft folds of her hairy crotch. 'I first used one on my seventeenth birthday and

51

since then I don't seem able to stop. Sometimes I think I must be over-sexed because, present company excepted, I haven't found very many cocks which really bring me off as well as a vibro! But perhaps you didn't know that God only created men because vibrators can't mow the lawn!'

Sir Stafford cleared his throat as he peered across to see the tip of the battery powered dildo, which was covered in a soft flesh coloured latex rubber, push itself between Angela's puffy cuntal lips.

'Tell me what turns you on about using a vibrator, my dear,' he said hoarsely whilst he unzipped his flies and fumbled inside the slit of his boxer shorts for his burgeon-ing shaft. He brought out his stubby, circumcised cock and slicked his hand up and down his twitching tool as he added: 'Do you play with yourself every night, you bad girl?'

'Not *every* night,' she conceded as she continued to tease herself by slipping the head of her imitation cock in and out of her love tunnel. 'And I don't want you to think that I don't enjoy a nice juicy cock inside my cunt because I do! Still, as I said it takes a lot to beat a good session with my King Dong vibrator. I like to start by lying back on the bed and then slowly stripping myself, using the vibro not just on my pussy but all over, starting with my cheeks. I love the feel of it buzzing all over me – especially when I move it further and further down. Of course, the last things to come off are my knickers because I like to run the vibrator all over the gusset until I get nice and wet. Then I know I'm ready to be fucked.'

She smiled seductively at the M.P. whose hand was now slicking furiously up and down his twitching tool and then went on: 'I slide that lovely hard stick into my cunny and begin to breathe hard as I jerk it in and out of my quim as I move my hips up and down. Honestly, it's often better than the real thing, the way it reaches all the way up my cunt and when I get really excited I often use two hands, pumping it in and out of my pussy, going faster and faster when I feel I'm close to a cum. I always climax with my vibrator, sometimes several times.

'Look, I'll show you,' said the randy secretary. She lay back on the bed whilst she jerked her plaything in and out of her moistening crack. 'This one you bought me is fabulous,' she panted as she masturbated at an ever-increasing speed, sliding the buzzing vibrator to and fro between the pouting lips of her pussy. 'It's got variable speed control and the head twists and turns all on its own.

'Oooh, that's great, I think I'm cumming,' she cried out. Still excitedly rubbing his short but thick truncheon, Sir Stafford leaped out of the chair and straddled her, just as an arc of spunk shot out of his cock to land directly in the cleft between Angela's generous bosoms. She dipped her fingers in the sticky pool of jism and smeared the creamy essence on her tits.

Then as she licked the salty liquid off her fingers the telephone rang and Sir Stafford leaned over to take the call. 'Yes, what is it, Mrs Paxford? I told you I didn't want to be disturbed,' he said irritably to his housekeeper who was on the other end of the line. 'Oh, I see, well that's different, please tell her I'll be down in a few moments.

'There's a girl from the College of Further Education downstairs who's come to pick up some papers from me,' he explained as he hauled himself off the bed and slid his shiny prick back inside his trousers. 'Don't go away, I'll only be a couple of minutes.'

'Don't worry, I'm not going anywhere,' said Angela lazily as the portly Sir Stafford hastily zipped up his trousers, put on his jacket and made his way to the door.

She lay back on the bed and wondered when the M.P.

would actually ask to stick his stubby shaft inside her sex slit for, up till now, he had done everything except actually fuck her. She grinned as she recalled how he had given her three crisp new ten pound notes to give him a pair of her scanty white panties which he wrapped round his bulging cock whilst he wanked himself off in his office.

The next day Sir Stafford had given her two more tenners and she had pulled her fist up and down his twitching tool whilst he groaned with pleasure. He must have needed this relief badly because he had come in under thirty seconds. This is money for old rope, she thought to herself, when for fifty pounds she had tugged down his trousers and underpants down in a flash and had licked and sucked his shaft whilst she gently squeezed his balls. Again, he had climaxed so quickly that Angela felt she could not ask him for a further present when he asked her to bend over a chair and lift up her skirt so that he could press his semi-erect wet cock against her wiggling bum cheeks.

There's no accounting for taste, she muttered as she picked up a copy of Sir Stafford's *Daily Mirror*. She read with interest that Scott Mackenzie's record *San Francisco* was now Top of the Pops, replacing The Beatles' *All You Need Is Love* which had now dropped into second place with Dave Davies's *Death of a Clown* in third place.

Angela turned the page to look at Gypsy Lionel's astrology column. Meanwhile, downstairs in Sir Stafford's study, Sharon was finding it extremely difficult to keep a straight face as Falmington's Member of Parliament stood at the side of his desk slipping rubber bands over half a dozen sets of printed documents. In his haste, Sir Stafford had not noticed that the zip fastener on his flies had broken and as he had not tucked his meaty shaft inside his boxer shorts, he was giving Sharon an occasional glimpse of his wedding tackle.

Should she tell him, she wondered, or is he deliberately showing me his cock like one of those stupid flashers who hung around the edge of her school's sports ground in the hope of exposing themselves to any unwary schoolgirl taking a short cut through a clump of trees to the pavilion. 'Take no notice of them, girls,' Miss Thomson, their angular headmistress had told her sixth form pupils. 'They only get their perverted pleasure if a girl shows her disgust or fright. My advice is to ignore them completely or, if they try and block your path, just look them straight in the eye and say loudly to attract the attention of anyone else walking nearby: "Put that thing away at once, do you hear!" and the man will simply slink away.'

Nevertheless, although Sharon decided to keep quiet about Sir Stafford's indiscretion – she reasoned that it was quite possible that Falmington's Member of Parliament was genuinely unaware that his flies were open – when he walked across the room to give her the sets of documents for Dr Teplin, he stumbled slightly. The bulbous knob of Sir Stafford's prick was now even more clearly visible through the open slit in the front of his trousers and so Sharon gave a perky smile and said: 'Sir Stafford, did you know that you're flying low?'

'Flying low?' he echoed blankly but when Sharon pointed wordlessly to his groin, his jaw dropped in horror and he frantically tried to tug up the zip, but only succeeded in breaking it completely. As he had forgotten to button up the catch at the top of his flies, his trousers gently slipped to the floor leaving his semi-erect shaft sticking lewdly out of the slit of his undershorts.

'Oh, I'm terribly sorry, I do beg your pardon Miss Shaw – please forgive me, I had no idea that I was um, oh dear, oh dear,' he gabbled as wild thoughts of a *News Of The World* headline of M.P. IN KINKY SEX STORM floated in front of his eyes. He saw himself desperately trying to explain away what had actually occurred at the next committee meeting of Falmington-On-Sea Conservative Association.

'That's alright, I've seen several cocks and they're all much of a muchness to me,' said Sharon with a shrug as Sir Stafford hastily shoved his shaft inside his boxer shorts. 'Personally, I happen to think that women's bodies are far sexier.'

'Do you?' said a pleasant female voice from the door and they both turned to the doorway where a barefoot Angela Amos, dressed in Sir Stafford's silk dressing gown stood leaning against the wall with an amused little smile playing around her lips.

'Cocks are okay and I love rubbing them when they're soft and seeing them swell up in my hand, but pussies are very pretty and far neater too, tucked out of sight under a bed of curly hair,' she mused as she closed the door behind her and plumped herself on the large sofa.

She looked at the stupefied backbencher and said to him with a note of reproach in her voice: 'Well now, aren't you going to introduce this nice girl to me?'

Sir Stafford muttered a few words and the two girls shook hands. 'I hope I haven't interrupted anything,' said Angela to Sharon. 'I only came down to get a Biro from my handbag when I looked in here and saw Stafford with his trousers round his ankles.'

'Oh, that was nothing to do with me,' said Sharon hurriedly. 'Please believe me, the zip on Sir Stafford's flies broke, that was all.'

Angela gave a throaty chuckle and patted the cushion next to her. She crooked her finger to beckon Sharon to sit down beside her and said: 'Don't worry, I believe you. Even this randy old goat isn't such a fast worker as all that. Mind you, Stafford flies his own private airplane and knowing him, I can tell you that he'd like nothing better than to show you his joystick.'

'Very droll, Angela, very droll,' grunted Sir Stafford
sarcastically although he was far from displeased by her
reference to his ability to fly his own aircraft. This often
impressed people when they learned of his prowess at
piloting his own single-engined Cherokee from an airstrip
on the outskirts of Falmington to his little country cottage
across the channel in Normandy.

'Still, as you've decided to honour Miss Shaw and
myself with your presence, why don't I get a bottle of
bubbly out of the fridge and we'll all have a drink. I know
it's a bit early in the day, but a nice ice-cold Buck's Fizz
goes down very nicely at any time.

'No, don't ring for Mrs Paxford, there's no need for her
to come up here,' he added quickly when he saw Angela
reach back to press the bell on the wall behind the sofa.
'She has enough on her hands at the moment. I'll pop in
to the kitchen and bring up a bottle of champagne and
some orange juice from the fridge if you'll get out some
glasses from the cocktail cabinet – but first, I'll go upstairs
and change my trousers!'

'That would be best,' agreed Angela and after he had
shut the door behind him Sharon remarked: 'Sir Stafford's a more considerate man than I would have given
him credit for, not wanting to give his housekeeper any
extra work. It only goes to show that you really can't
judge a book by its cover.'

'I wouldn't go as far as that,' said Angela darkly. 'The
old bugger is only worried that Mrs Paxford comes in and
sees more than she should, if you get my meaning. He's
barmy if he thinks she doesn't know what we've been
getting up to in his bedroom, especially when he reminds
her to make up a jug of cold custard in the fridge before
she leaves.'

'Cold custard?'

'Yes, he dips his prick in it and then I wash it off with my tongue – or sometimes I pour the custard over my pussy and then he licks it out of my cunt.'

Sharon wrinkled her nose as she digested this information. 'Do you mean to say that Sir Stafford makes you do this as part of the job——'

'Oh no, to be fair, Stafford's a terrible letch but when he's not a bad lad and accepts that when a girl says "no" she means what she says,' Angela interrupted. She opened the cocktail cabinet and took out three fluted champagne glasses. 'He's never tried to force me to do anything I didn't want to and he's generous enough when he wants me to give him any special after-hours services. Actually, I rather enjoy giving him a hand job but if he wants to put an extra tenner in my pay packet at the end of the week for a couple of quick hand jobs in his office, I'm not going to object too much.'

'But doesn't your boy friend get upset about this arrangement?' enquired Sharon and Angela shrugged her shoulders and answered: 'No, he doesn't mind. You see Timmy's in the Navy and he's been away since February and won't be back till November. Well, we write to each other every fortnight because Timmy's stationed at the naval base in Malta and so from what he tells me in his letters, I know that he's not been living like a monk.

'And nor have I been living like a nun,' she added as Sir Stafford came back in carrying a bottle of champagne and a jug of orange juice on a silver tray. ' "What's sauce for the goose is sauce for the gander," I said to him when we said goodbye at Southampton. "If you want to have a poke whilst you're away, then you mustn't expect me not to turn away the chance of a good fuck".'

Sir Stafford picked up the last few words and raised his eyebrows as he carefully began to uncork the champagne. 'What's that about a good fuck, Angela?' he said in a fruity voice as he popped open the bottle. 'Are you talking about me again?'

'Don't flatter yourself,' Angela replied, holding out her glass for Sir Stafford to fill although when she saw him scowl, she added kindly: 'Now then, don't get all upset, you're by no means the worst lover I've ever had. Mind you, with so many girls on the Pill, the men have never had it so good. Well, good luck to them, but I just wish that there were more boys around who have some appreciation of the finer points of fucking.

'For instance, I can get turned on just by seeing a well-hung lad standing nude especially if his dangling cock hangs below his balls, but so many men think that just putting their pricks inside a pussy is enough. Well, it isn't! I don't know what turns you on, Sharon, but some good-old fashioned passionate kissing gets me in the mood.'

'Oh yes, me too,' Sharon readily agreed as Sir George topped up her glass of champagne with a dash of fresh orange juice. Then looking Angela straight in the eye she went on: 'I'm not anti-men, but I've found that on the whole, girls tend to be more considerate to their partners in bed. I live with a girl named Denise and she's the most wonderful lover that anyone could ever want.'

A bulge began to form in Sir Stafford's crotch as he poured himself a drink and sat down opposite her. 'How very interesting,' he said huskily. 'Do tell me more, I might get some valuable tips on how to be a better lover.'

'Well, you just must find out what pleases your partner and it all falls into place from there,' answered Sharon as she settled back on the sofa. 'For example, Denise understands how it takes me time to get turned on. She knows that I love to be undressed whilst we're kissing, and how I adore the way she slowly unbuttons my blouse and slides it off my shoulders whilst we're necking and how, still with our tongues in each other's mouths, she fondles my tits before unzipping my skirt and taking it off before pulling down my panties.

'Of course, by now I'm doing the same to her and this really builds up the tension. Then it's nice if we stand up and hug and rub our bodies against each other for a while before we begin to make it in bed. There, she'll kiss and lick the insides of my legs all the way up my body to my face, purposefully not having contact with my tits and cunt. By now she's brought me to the peak and when she goes down on me I begin cumming as soon as she slips her tongue inside my honeypot.'

'Yes, I've yet to meet a guy who can eat pussy like a girl,' sighed Angela as she downed her Bucks Fizz and Sir Stafford moved across briskly to refill her glass. 'And the best cunny sucker I've ever come across was an attractive young girl called Clare who I met at a party I went to a few weeks ago in Chelsea. I'd ricked my back playing tennis and tried to get rid of the pain by having a few drinks but this didn't help very much, although it did make me feel more relaxed.

'Anyhow, when I mentioned it to Clare she said she'd give me a relaxing massage so we went upstairs to one of the bedrooms and whilst she searched around for some baby oil in the bathroom, on her instruction I undressed and lay naked face down on the bed. Well, she came back and spread a little baby oil on my back and began smoothing it into my skin with her fingertips. Now I was a wee bit concerned that she was a lezzie but gradually I unwound as she gave me a great massage with no funny business, just smoothing her hands up and down my back. I could almost feel the pain and tension seeping out of me.

'Then she tapped me on the shoulder and told me to roll over and I kept my eyes closed as she spread-eagled my legs and started massaging my thighs. I slowly became aware that the idea of this pretty girl looking at my pussy was turning me on – and somehow Clare knew this because she slipped her hands up to my breasts and began to rotate the tips of my nipples in her palms. "Does that feel good?" she asked softly and before I replied, I opened my eyes and saw that she had also taken off her clothes and was kneeling between my legs in the nude!'

'I managed to croak out "Yes, it's marvellous," and it was as if my whole body was turning to jelly, starting in my cunt and spreading out in great warm waves. I came in lovely long surges and I had to put my hand over my mouth to muffle the sounds that I couldn't control.

'As I began to come down, Clare started to stroke my inner thighs between my pussy and my bum and then finally she touched my clitty and I came again then and there, twisting and bucking as a huge orgasm shuddered through me.

"My! You are a sexy girl," said Clare and then she leaned forward to lick my erect titties and worked her mouth tantalisingly down to my juicy crack as she went on: "It's been some time since I've worked on such a good-looking girl as you."

'As soon as her tongue was pushed up inside me I shuddered and just lay back and enjoyed the sensations as she carried on lapping up my love juices, noisily slurping from my cunny. She rubbed my clitty with her thumb and this time the orgasm just seemed to last forever and I felt drained and exhausted afterwards – but when I got up and stretched across the bed to grab my knickers, I didn't feel the slightest twinge!'

There was silence for a moment and then Sharon giggled and said: 'So is this how you discovered that you swung both ways?'

'Not exactly, although now I realise that if I dig

someone enough, male or female, then anything goes,' Angela replied as she suggestively stroked the blonde girl's knee.

She said nothing but cocked her head and looked at Angela with a saucy smile playing around her lips. Sir Stafford blurted out hoarsely: 'By God, what about it, girls? I'd give anything to see you two get it together.'

Sharon was tempted by this suggestion, but when she heard the mid-day chimes of the grandfather clock in the hall she remembered that she had a twelve-thirty date with her friends and so shook her head and replied: 'Sorry, Sir Stafford, I wouldn't mind but it would have to be another time. I have an appointment back at the college and I'll be late if I don't make a move soon. However, I have your phone number and I'll give you a call and perhaps we can fix up something later this week.

'Which reminds me, may I please use your phone to order a taxi?' she concluded.

Sir Stafford Stiffkey M.P. sighed sadly as he pointed to the telephone on a side table near the door. 'Of course you may,' he said courteously, making a mental note to call this sexy young blonde at her office first thing in the morning. 'It's been a pleasure meeting you, hasn't it, Angela? You must come back soon to Austin Lodge.'

Chapter Two

On The Job

Later, over a sandwich and glass of wine at a nearby pub, Sharon related with some relish the story of the strange goings-on to Denise Cochran and the two French boys. Unfortunately, just as she was coming to the end of her anecdote, a brisk sea breeze suddenly blew up and sent a grey bank of clouds scudding across the sky. Then Pierre Truchet remembered that he had left a half-finished letter to his parents in the library and he left the other three to walk back to the college, retrieve and finish it off and then post it before rejoining them.

Rather than go back to work, the others walked back to the Frenchmen's flat where Marc poured out generous measures of calvados for the girls before disappearing into the kitchen to put on the kettle.

'You English make such a fuss about your politicians' private lives,' he commented affably after he returned with three mugs of freshly made real coffee. 'I am sure that if a newspaper published a story about how this girl Angela was having an affair with Sir Stafford, the poor chap would be forced to resign his seat, although it's no secret that he and his wife separated more than four years ago and have lived completely separate lives since then. And even if Lady Stiffkey agreed to a divorce, it appears that a large section of his electorate would be shocked and disgusted if they were told that their M.P. was fucking his secretary. I must say that I find this all terribly hypocritical – do these people never make love themselves, or do they think that it is wrong to enjoy oneself in the bedroom?'

'They probably do, Marc,' grinned Denise as she took hold of her mug. 'Some European journalist once wrote that the Continentals have sex lives and the English have hot water bottles! Still, I think that attitudes have changed recently. You know, Swinging London and all that. Why, the other day I heard some French dress designer say on the radio that London is the only place to be for the jet set and has become the Mecca for Parisians who are tired of Paris. I forget the guy's name but he was someone famous – do you get a morning paper? I'll see if what he said was reported.'

She leaned forward to look for herself but as she did so some coffee spilled out from her mug and over her skirt.

'Oh fuck it!' she swore as she stood up and placed the mug on a side table.

'Have you burned yourself?' asked Marc anxiously but Denise shook her head. 'No, thank goodness, but look at the stain on my skirt.'

'Don't worry, that'll come out if we wash it straight away,' said Sharon comfortingly. 'Take the skirt off and I'll see to it right now. Marc, I presume you do keep some washing powder here, don't you?'

'In the cupboard underneath the sink,' he answered, trying to tear his eyes away from Denise who was already stepping out of her skirt to reveal her glorious long legs and deliciously firm bum cheeks which were covered only by a tiny pair of bikini panties which had ridden into the crack of her bottom. 'Let me do it though. At the same time I can wash this sweater and get out the stain from the wine which Pierre accidently spilt over me at lunchtime.'

Sharon chuckled and said: 'Well, take it off and I'll do it for you, it's no trouble. We'll have to let the garments soak for a little while and then I'll give them both a good scrub.'

'Well, if you're sure, I'd be very grateful,' he said as he pulled his sweater over his head and exposed his broad chest which was matted with fine brown hair. 'Now, who would like a little more calvados?'

Twenty minutes later, Denise's skirt and Marc's sweater were hanging on a line strung across the bath whilst the young Frenchman found himself on the sofa slumped between the two girls. The apple brandy they had been drinking steadily since arriving at the flat coupled with the wine which they had imbibed at the pub had loosened their tongues. When Denise ran her fingers through the hairs on Marc's chest, she absently murmured: 'Isn't this supposed to be a sign of virility?'

'What is?' demanded Marc as he slid his arm around her shoulders and pressed her closer to him. 'A hairy chest?'

'Yes, I must admit it does exude an aura of masculinity,' Denise added as she made a patterned ring of concentric circles around his nipples. 'It's funny that men's tits aren't as sensitive as ours.'

'That is our misfortune,' he replied with a smile as she rolled his nipples between her fingers. 'Some men find it a turn-on to have their girl-friends play with their tits but, as far as I'm concerned, it would be a hundred times more enjoyable if you would let me do to you what you are doing to me.'

'No, that is wrong, a thousand times more enjoyable,' he whispered into her ear. Denise shivered with excitement as she felt a familiar tingling in her crotch and a picture flashed through her mind of Marc Ribeaux lying naked on the floor in front of her. Suddenly she wanted to clutch hold of his stiff rock-hard cock and impale herself on the hot, throbbing shaft.

But did she want to be fucked, she asked herself, as Marc pulled her head gently towards his own? It had been three weeks since she had been fucked by Murray Lupowitz, her former editorial colleague at Chelmsford and Parrish. But now he had gone to work in Argentina and would not be back in England for at least another six months. Except for a brief fling with Murray, during the year Denise had only shared her bed with other girls – but there was no doubt that she was attracted by the handsome young Frenchman.

Before she could think of an answer, Marc had covered her lips with his own and kissed her. She could taste the coffee on his tongue as he explored the inner cavern of her mouth. Their tongues met and danced like passionate partners around each other whilst Denise threw off the shackles of any remaining inhibitions and flung her arms around his neck.

'I think I'll just see how those clothes are drying off,' Sharon said hastily as she heaved herself off the sofa. Marc's hands found the top of Denise's shirt and wiggled in between the buttonholes to caress her breasts, but he let out a whimpering little cry of frustration when she tore her mouth away and pushed him away with her palms against his bare chest.

Damn, I've gone too far too fast, thought Marc and he swallowed hard and said apologetically: 'I'm sorry, Denise, I don't know what came over me.'

She looked up at him with a saucy smile and then kissed his cheek as she murmured: 'There's nothing to be sorry for, you silly boy. I just want to take off this shirt before it gets creased!'

His face brightened as Denise stood up and swiftly divested herself of the shirt and her bra. Marc caught his breath as he stared at her luscious big breasts which jiggled so enticingly in front of him.

With a low growl, Marc pulled her back onto the sofa and they slipped back with ease into their embrace. He cupped her breasts, squeezing the creamy soft flesh and making her gasp with excitement as he rubbed his thumbs on her elongated tawny nipples. Then Denise lifted her bottom to allow him to tug down her panties and she moaned as he placed his hands on her moistening mound and began to massage her pussy lips with his finger whilst with the other he told hold of her own soft hand and placed it firmly on the huge bulge in his lap. Her whole body tingled when she felt the thick, rigid rod pressing against her fingers and she rubbed it from the outside of his trousers, caressing his knob through the thin fabric.

'*Mon Dieu*,' he gasped throatily as she unzipped his flies and released his enormous erection which sprung up through the slit of his undershorts. She clutched the warm, hard column in her fist and squeezed it, moving her hand slowly up and down whilst Marc pressed the tip of his forefinger directly into her squishy cunt. He looked into the deep liquid submission of her warm, brown eyes and again their mouths locked together into a fervent tongue-to-tongue encounter.

Then for a short time he withdrew his finger from her pussy to stroke her pouting love lips, his fingertips playing and teasing inside her soft, curly bush whilst she bucked her groin up and down against his hand to increase the pleasure. In response he began to rub his forefinger up and down the length of her damp crack.

She groaned with pleasure as he finger-fucked her with the utmost gentleness, gliding his finger inside her cunt and making her clitty swell with anticipation.

'Oooh, you naughty thing,' panted Denise as the heat between her thighs reached boiling point. Marc slipped a second and then a third finger into her wet slit, his long, sensitive fingers groping deep inside her cunny, finding her most hidden nooks. She trembled with erotic passion as he continued to slide his finger in and out of her churning love channel, now finding her erect fleshy clitty and using his thumb to massage the vibrating little bud.

'Please, Marc, please,' breathed the aroused girl, not even sure what she was asking for when the Frenchman removed his fingers from her cunt and removed her hand from his cock. He slid himself down on his knees and positioned himself between her thighs. For a moment he looked up at her and then he buried his face inside her glossy wet bush and ground her cunt up against his mouth as he took her erect clitty between his lips and flicked it on the very tip with his tongue until her orgasm began to build and grow in strength as he sucked with growing intensity. She clutched at his head and screamed with joy as he brought her off, flicking his tongue at a great speed in and out of her juicy pussy as she orgasmed, her hips bucking as a flood of love juice came tumbling out of her cunt, soaking his face.

Denise's trembling body relaxed as the tension snapped with her spend, but the sight of Marc's bulging, veined shaft as she lay across the sofa whilst he clambered up on top of her soon fired the lusty girl once again and she automatically spread her legs wide apart. She grabbed hold of his cock and guided it into the red chink between the pouting love lips and he went right inside her, sliding directly into her quim on the juicy slick of cuntal juice.

A wild primal snarl escaped from Marc's throat as he sank his shaft forward until their pubic hairs were enmeshed. They bounced up and down on the sofa as he pulled her cunny lips open to ease the passage of his glistening wet prick. He made love to her with a fervent passion, his cock throbbing violently as it slewed in and out of her sopping cunny, trying to keep his strokes reasonably paced. But the sight of Denise's creamy ripe breasts excited him so much that he fucked the beautiful willing girl faster and faster with all the energy that he could muster.

'Y-e-s-s-s! Y-e-s-s! Y-e-s-s!' she cried out, writhing in uncontrolled delight as Marc's buttocks rose and fell, his muscular torso shuddering whilst he pounded his veiny truncheon harder and harder into her cunny, rapidly transporting Denise to ever higher peaks of pleasure. She screamed out with joy as a quick series of pre-cum sensations crackled through her body and she jerked her hips upwards to pump her creaming cunny against his twitching tool, the clenching muscles of her cunny gripping Marc's cock as wave after wave of sheer ecstasy washed over her and she squeezed his shaft powerfully as she exploded into a tremendous orgasm.

Now Marc felt an awesome climax building up as his balls smacked against her beautiful backside. He lunged forward one final time into her dripping crack and jetted a sticky fountain of spunk which splattered against the walls of her love funnel, sending yet a further round of erotic ripples of bliss out from Denise's cunt as she milked dry his pulsing prick. He collapsed down on her, barely able to catch his breath.

Only now did they hear the sound of heavy breathing. Marc turned his head to see Sharon standing only a few feet away from them, stark naked with her long legs parted, fingering her pussy with one hand whilst massaging her breasts with the other.

Then Denise saw her friend playing with herself. She wriggled out from underneath Marc and, sinking down on her knees in front of the blonde girl's flaxen muff, she cried out: 'Oh, you poor dear, let me finish you off.'

Marc's jaw dropped open as he watched Sharon take out her hand from her golden bush and offer her fingers, which were coated in pussy juice, to Denise who eagerly licked them clean. Then she embedded her tousled head between Sharon's thighs and licked and lapped on her sweet cunny. Sharon panted: 'Aaaah! Don't stop, Denise darling, lick my clitty and make me come like you did this morning!'

Like you did this morning, repeated Marc to himself as he craned his neck to look closely at the two girls who were now oblivious to anything but the sensuous feel of their love-making. He knew that a fortnight ago Denise had moved out of the Royal Windsor Hotel to share a flat with Sharon, but he had no idea that they were lovers. Still, this was their business, he muttered with a typical Gallic shrug as he hauled himself up, and perhaps like her friend, Sharon also liked to fuck men.

There's only one way to find out, Marc decided. He sat up, kicked off his shoes and pulled off his socks and then his trousers and pants which he had tugged down to his feet before he began fucking Denise. Now as naked as the girls, he padded to Sharon who was standing with her head thrown back, her hands clutching Denise's head. He murmured in her ear: 'You'll be more comfortable lying down on the sofa.'

'Thanks, Marc,' she said gratefully as she bent down to kiss Denise's head. 'Did you hear what Marc said, darling? Let's move to the sofa and I can lie down whilst you bring me off.'

In a trice Sharon was lying on her back with her thighs clasped round the other girl's neck as Denise lifted her pretty face and muttered: 'M'mm, what a succulent smell of pussy! I'm really going to enjoy licking out your delicious little cunt!'

As Marc looked on at the erotic sight of Denise's head

bobbing between Sharon's thighs, his cock began to thicken and he pulled back his foreskin and kneaded the uncapped mushroom crown until his shaft was sticking up against his flat belly, as hard as a drill. Then he moved forward purposefully until his groin was level with Sharon's head and he pulled her head round to look at his swollen prick. Her eyes widened and then without ado she licked her lips and kissed Marc's gleaming knob which glistened with the evidence of his wet excitement. Then she took his cock in her right hand and moved her head slightly forward to run her tongue around the ridge of the smooth wide dome of his helmet. Slowly she started to move her head back and forth and, as she drew breath, she inhaled his musky masculine odour when his knob slid across the back of her throat.

'Aiee! *C'est merveilleux, ma chèrie,*' Marc gasped as Sharon began to lick his prick as if it were an ice-cream cornet, teasing her tongue up and down the sides of his hot velvet skinned shaft. She gurgled with satisfaction and transferred her attentions to his balls, taking each of them into her mouth and nudging them with her tongue whilst her fingers fondled his quivering cock in her hand.

Sharon released his balls and moved her lips back to his cock which she took deep inside her mouth. Her hand cupped his balls as she feasted on his pulsating prick, sucking hard with her cheeks hollowing as her tongue glided back and forth along the sensitive underside of his throbbing column.

Marc cradled her head in his hands, holding it gently as he felt the spunk rushing up from his balls as Sharon's eager sucking worked its magic. Now her hand jerked up and down his shaft as she swirled her tongue around his knob which soon brought him to the crisis and he spurted profusely down her throat. Marc groaned loudly as Sharon gulped down his sticky emission with relish, gobbling deeply, sliding her mouth backwards and forwards, pumping with her hand on her shaft and rubbing his knob on the roof of her mouth until he pulled his softening shaft from between her lips.

In the meantime, Denise had busied herself in licking and lapping around the teenager's fluffy blonde bush and now Sharon groaned as she felt Denise's tongue probe between her love lips and a great shudder of delight passed through her body as the older girl closed her warm lips over the fleshy bud of her clitty.

'Aaaah! Here I go!' Sharon cried out and her hips squirmed as Denise sucked forcefully on her sopping cunny. The love juice poured out of her cunt, wetting Denise's face and dripping down onto the cushion of the sofa until, her belly rippling in spasm after spasm, she achieved a delicious climax under the hungry working of Denise's lips and tongue.

Marc slumped down on his knees and kissed Sharon's tawny nipples before laying his head on Sharon's flat belly and the three of them lay silent for a while, recovering from their delightful but exhausting labours.

Denise was the first to come to her senses. 'Come on, you two, we can't stay here all afternoon,' she said briskly. 'We must get dressed before Pierre comes back.'

'There's no need to worry about Pierre. He would be only too happy to find two beautiful naked girls in his living room!' said Marc sleepily, but Denise wriggled herself up from between Sharon's legs and delivered a light slap on his bottom.

'Maybe so, but Sharon and I have work to do,' declared Denise as she slipped on her knickers. 'Actually, you might be able to help us, Marc. We need to speak to Pierre's friend Belinda Blisswood as soon as possible. Do you know if she is working at the Berkeley today?'

'Yes, as it happens Belinda was here last night but

Pierre took her home quite early because she had to begin work at eight o'clock this morning,' he replied, glancing at his watch. 'But she'll probably be leaving there quite soon. Why don't you ring the hotel and see if you can catch her. The phone is in the hall and the hotel's number is Falmington 6000.'

'Thanks, Marc, you're a star,' said Denise gratefully, zipping up her skirt as she hurried out to make the call.

'Is everything all right?' Marc asked Sharon as she sat up and playfully flipped his dangling member over his thigh.

'Oh yes, we just want some information about the hotel from her,' she answered absently, squeezing his shaft until it started to twitch and thicken in her hand. 'My goodness, Monsieur Ribeaux, your prick is insatiable. You've fucked Denise and I've sucked you off – surely that's enough sex for one afternoon. Haven't you heard the old English saying that you can have too much of a good thing?'

His cock continued to swell as Sharon pulled down his foreskin and exposed the rosy knob as she began to masturbate him with her skilful fingers and Marc said hoarsely: 'I'm not sure whether I would agree with that, especially if you continue rubbing your hand up and down my cock.'

'Well just say the word if you would like me to stop,' she giggled and Marc shook his head vigorously and exclaimed: 'No, no, it's lovely but——'

'But we don't have time for any more rumpy pumpy,' cut in Denise as she came back from the hall. 'Sharon, I spoke to Belinda and she was just about to leave, but I asked her to wait for us. So leave Marc's cock alone and get dressed, love. I said we'd be with Belinda in about twenty minutes.'

'Spoilsport!' Sharon complained but she released

Marc's cock and picked up her panties from the carpet. She planted a light kiss on his uncapped bell-end before she straightened up and said: 'Thank you for a lovely time, Marc, will we see you at College tomorrow?'

He nodded sorrowfully as he looked down at his aching stiffstander and then with a downcast expression on his face he glanced up piteously at Denise who sighed and said: 'All right, I'll put your prick out of its misery whilst Denise gets dressed.'

She dropped to her knees and took hold of his cock as she twirled her tongue up and down his shaft before opening her mouth and sucking in his helmet into her mouth. Slowly at first she began to bob her head up and down on his thick truncheon, encompassing inch after inch of his palpitating pole as she slid her hands underneath his tightening balls. He jerked his hips upwards in time to fuck her sweet mouth in long slow strokes and even though, as Sharon had reminded him, Marc had orgasmed twice during the previous torrid hour, his cock soon signalled that a third gush of spunk was travelling up from his scrotum to his twitching shaft.

He growled as the climax neared and he shot his load down Denise's throat although this time only a trickle of creamy seed spouted out of his cock. Nonetheless, Denise was quite satisfied to swallow the reduced amount of salty clean jism and licked the last blobs from the tip of his shaft until his penis wilted and shrivelled down to a weary limpness.

Fifteen minutes later Denise and Sharon were sitting in a cafe next door to the Berkeley Hotel with Belinda Blisswood who was listening with growing excitement as the girls explained the purpose of her visit.

'So there we are,' Denise concluded quietly, making sure that they could not be overheard. 'Shane will book in under the name of Michael Reynolds on Friday night and it would be wonderful if you could find out which room he's staying in. I've no idea who this Louise is who he's come down to see and whether she's going to meet him in the hotel, but I'd prefer to meet Shane before she does or he'll be so busy screwing her that he won't open the door for anybody.'

'Leave it to me, I'll see if we know what time Shane's supposed to be arriving,' promised Belinda firmly. 'Then we can make sure we're around to collar him. Gosh, this is so exciting! I never managed to get near Shane at the concert and staff weren't allowed into the party that Mr Swaffer gave for him afterwards.

'I'll do *anything,* to meet him,' she said dramatically. Denise gave an ironic smile and remarked: 'You may well have to, love, but don't worry, we won't tell poor old Pierre that he's probably facing a lonesome weekend.'

Belinda shrugged her shoulders. 'I'm afraid that's tough luck on Pierre,' she remarked. 'He's a nice lad and I like him a lot but I'll never have another chance to fuck Shane Hammond. Pierre will just have to lick his own dick on Saturday night.'

'Gosh, can Pierre really suck his own cock?' Sharon asked with interest and Belinda laughed as she shook her head. ''fraid not, he would need a far more spine back and a much longer cock. I believe that some men can do it, though. You know Michael, the stylist at *Hair Today*? He once told me that not only could a friend of his do it but that this chap actually preferred it to fucking.'

'Good grief, why was that?' enquired Denise and Belinda answered with a giggle: 'He said it gave him a chance to meet a better class of girl!'

Sharon looked at her crossly and grumbled: 'Oh, what a rotten swizz! I didn't realise you were having us on! I was just reminding myself to ask Michael for the name of his friend!'

'Sorry to disappoint you,' apologised Belinda and then she grinned and went on: 'Anyhow, I didn't honestly think that either of you were into big cocks, don't you prefer pussies instead?'

'Not necessarily,' Sharon corrected her as she wagged a reproving finger. 'Denise and I swing both ways so we get the best of all the action – and I'm sure you'll agree that a big cock is a guarantee of a good time.'

'It isn't always,' corrected Belinda as she finished her lemonade and leaning forward over the table, she dropped her voice and continued: 'You know Steven Williams, that radio producer who was lecturing on how to get into broadcasting at your college last week? Well, he was staying here and he fucked me beautifully even though he doesn't have the most massive cock I've ever seen.

'I've sampled a few tools in my time and more often than not I've preferred a smaller shaft to a gigantic rammer. There were these two young waiters at the Berkeley last year who I fancied. Do you remember Garry and Neil, Sharon, they took us out for a drink one night? Well, Garry was hung like a donkey. You've never seen such an enormous cock, but it stretched me to the limit and it was far more enjoyable having Neil's six-inch shaft my pussy. Once he'd slipped his shaft inside me it wiggled around wonderfully in my cunt and I don't think I've ever come so quickly.

She sighed heavily and concluded: 'If only men would realise that it's not the size of the ship that counts, it's the motion of the ocean, although I must admit that when I go down to the beach, the sight of a good-looking lad with a big hard-on bulging out of his swimming trunks does turn me on.'

'Well, Pierre had better look to his laurels or is he well hung?' asked Denise and Belinda chuckled and said: 'Oh, I've no complaints, but variety is the spice of life! Don't tell Pierre, but in fact I had a marvellous fuck with a chap named Jack Dennison who I met in the bar the other evening. He was only staying overnight as he had driven his elderly parents down all the way from Glasgow to stay for a fortnight at Falmington and he decided to stay overnight before setting off back home.

'To be frank, we both had a bit too much to drink and were pretty sloshed when I went up to his room with him, but when we started to kiss I could feel his stiff cock pressing against me. Although he wasn't the most broad-shouldered guy in the world, he was damned strong because without any effort he scooped me up in his arms and carried me over to the bed. I helped him take off my dress and after he unhooked my bra he lay down beside me and began tonguing my nipples till they were standing up like two little red pyramids.

'Jack was one of those men who knew which buttons to press and when to press them. When we kissed, his tongue slid between my teeth and just at the right time he ripped off my panties and thrust his finger into my wet cunt, fingering my clitty till I came and had an orgasm which felt as if there were an earthquake underneath the hotel.

'I was putty in his hands and I couldn't wait for him to tear off his clothes. I pulled down his pants myself and grasped hold of his stiff thick shaft whilst he put his head down and began sucking on my titties. My pussy was already moist and tingling with anticipation when Jack grabbed a pillow and, slipping it under my bum to raise my hips, he bent his head down to give my soaking cunt a loving wet kiss.

"Fuck me, Jack, I want your cock inside me," I

whispered fiercely and he raised himself over me as I spread my legs and reached out to guide his throbbing tool to the target. He eased his veiny shaft into me and immediately started to fuck me in long, pumping strokes. It felt like I was being turned inside out each time he pulled back and it was just heavenly when he pushed forward.'

'Sounds like he was a bloody good fuck,' commented Denise and a blissful smile spread over Belinda's face as she answered: 'Jack was perhaps the very best. He had this amazing technique to excite me. I started to come almost as soon as he started ramming his shaft a little bit faster into my soaking cunt and I loved the way his balls slapped against my bum each time he went in to the hilt. Honestly, in about thirty seconds he had me bucking upwards to meet his downward thrusts, and I was almost bouncing off the bed with the incredible force of his fucking.

'When I felt my climax coming on I spurred him on by panting in his ear: "Come on, Jack, come on. Shoot your load inside my juicy pussy, I love the feeling of spunk splashing against the walls of my cunt".

'This worked a treat and my back arched upwards as I thrust myself against him whilst Jack groaned and I could feel every contraction of his cock inside my quim whilst he shot his load, flooding my cunny with his creamy jism as we came together.'

She paused to mop her brow as she gave a husky chuckle and went on: 'As Jack pulled out his shrunken cock from my pussy he collapsed on the bed beside me and panted: "Thank God I don't have to leave Falmington till about ten tomorrow morning because I don't think I'd be in any fit condition to make an early start!"

'Then he rolled over and kissed me and said that I was a terrific lover and I kissed him back and returned the compliment as I really liked this man. Luckily my parents were away so I didn't have to go home and Jack fucked me twice more before we went to sleep and in the morning I woke him up with a nice juicy blow job.'

Sharon whistled softly and remarked: 'Wow, you obviously had a great night! I'm surprised Jack had the strength to drive back to Glasgow.'

'Yes, Jack was quite shagged out and it was just as well he broke his journey to spend a night with an old friend of his who lives near Manchester,' said Belinda with a grin. 'We keep in touch though and send each other naughty letters every month. Jack's the field sales manager in Scotland for a stationery company and he writes to me on this new scented notepaper.'

She rummaged in her bag and brought out an envelope which she passed to Sharon. 'I heard from him only yesterday. Here, you can read what he has to say whilst I go back to the hotel and see when Shane – oops, sorry Denise, I mean "Mr Reynolds" – is expected. It'll only take me a minute but as we don't want anyone asking any awkward questions, I'll wait till the coast is clear.'

'Thanks, love,' said Sharon as she opened the unsealed envelope and took out Jack Dennison's letter. 'We'll wait here for you. Here, move your chair round, Denise and you can look at it with me. Somehow I don't think it's the kind of letter to be read aloud!'

She sorted the sheets of perfumed paper out and the girls read:

Dear Belinda,

Lovely to hear from you Monday and that you're having fine weather down in Falmington. It hasn't been too bad here but I can't wait to get away on my summer holiday next week with my friend Dave, the taxi driver from Newton Mearns I've mentioned before to you.

We had a great time last weekend. Dave and I had been invited to a party in Edinburgh on Saturday night, but as the weather was so good and as Dave and I sit on our backsides in our cars all week, we decided to drive across to Edinburgh on Saturday afternoon and have a good walk round Holyrood Park. We took our clothes for the party in a wee suitcase as we could always go into one of the big hotels to wash and change in the men's room.

Well, as Dave's a keen photographer, we walked all the way through Queen's Drive to Duddington and then all the way up to Arthur's Seat. It's a stiff climb but at the top you're over eight hundred feet over the city and it's well worth doing if you ever come to Edinburgh (which even as a Glaswegian, I must tell you is well worth doing!), especially in August during the Festival.

Anyhow, Dave took his photographs and we had just started to make our way down when we saw these two pretty girls dressed only in athletic tops and running shorts sitting on a small hillock of earth some fifty feet away. I was admiring the well-stacked figure of the taller girl, who was blonde with a lovely tanned skin, when she called out to us in an American accent: 'Hi there, I wonder if you guys would be kind enough to give us a hand?'

Dave and I only had time to exchange a quick glance before we almost broke our necks to scramble across to where the girls were sitting. 'What's the trouble, ma'am?' I asked and she told me that her friend had twisted her ankle and couldn't put any weight on her foot. She needed someone else to help get her down to the bottom of the mountain.

She told us that they were actresses with small parts in a new play being put on by an American theatre company at the Assembly Rooms and she anxiously added: 'We must start making a move soon or we'll be late for the four-thirty press call.'

'Don't fret, my wee hen, Jack and I will help out, no problem,' said Dave soothingly and we helped Karen, who was a pretty slender little thing with deep brown sensuous eyes and dark brown hair, to her feet.

'You're no weight at all, climb up on my back and I'll piggy-back you down the hill,' I said to her and she gave me a lovely wide smile and said: 'Are you sure? I'm not that light, last time I was on the scales I topped one hundred and ten pounds.'

I smiled back at her and told her that if she were too heavy for me then my friend would take over or she could perch on both our shoulders so that we would share her weight. 'My name's Jack, by the way, and this is Dave,' I said and she told me that her name was Tessa and that the blonde girl's name was Karen.

'We're from the Sharadski Theatre School in San Francisco,' explained Tessa. I bent forward and Dave and Karen helped hoist her on to my back and she wrapped her arms round my neck. 'Here we go,' I said cheerfully. 'Shall we take the scenic route?'

Tessa wasn't too heavy but after five minutes I thought I might have to stop and ask Dave to help me, but then I got my second wind and I carried her all the way till we reached St Leonard's Lane. Then we rested for a couple of minutes and when the girls thanked us again I said that it would be my pleasure to drive them up to the Assembly Rooms.

'We couldn't possibly put you to all that trouble, I'm sure there'll be a taxi coming along in a moment,' said Tessa but naturally I said I wouldn't hear of it

and told her: 'Don't be silly, it'll be my pleasure, you two stay here with Dave and I'll bring the car round. It's only parked at the bottom of Bernard Terrace.'

Well, to cut a long story short, I drove the girls up to the Assembly Rooms where we stayed for the press conference. Afterwards the girls insisted on inviting us back for a drink at their hotel over the road – not that we needed much persuading! We got on very well and then Tessa winced and groaned: 'Damn it, my ankle's getting painful again. Jack, do you think you could help me up to my room?'

'Of course I will,' I said gallantly and, leaning heavily on my shoulder, Tessa hobbled out to the lifts. When we were safely inside her bedroom she hopped through to the bathroom and then returned in a minute or two and threw herself down on the bed. She smiled up at me and said: 'Sorry to be a nuisance, Jack, but I've now got cramp in my thighs. Would you like to massage them for me?'

I gave a nervous little gulp because I know nothing about first aid but I wasn't going to pass up this opportunity! I knelt down on the bed next to her. Of course, as soon as I touched her bare silky smooth skin, my prick sprang to life and I was slightly embarrassed about the tented protrusion between my legs as I carefully caressed her soft, warm thighs.

Tessa lay back and closed her eyes whilst I stroked her and when she twisted to get herself into a more comfortable position and smoothed her hands over her jiggling breasts, my cock began aching to jump out of my pants as I realised that Tessa had taken off her bra. Then I realised that she was now sitting up with her eyes open with a saucy look on her pretty face.

'I'll bet you could use a massage too after carrying

me all that way,' said Tessa, staring at the bulge in my trousers, but I needn't have felt embarrassed because she scrambled to her knees and pulled me down to lie next to her and kissed me, her nimble fingers rubbing my straining shaft whilst I reached down and fondled her breasts.

We undressed each other whilst we writhed around on the bed and we soon found ourselves in a glorious sixty-nine position with Tessa's bum between my lips whilst she cupped my balls in her hand as she gobbled my glistening swollen helmet into her mouth. I curled my tongue, stiffened it and then flicked it around the rim of her wrinkled little arsehole. This thrilled Tessa who squealed with pleasure and then wrapped her lips tightly round my cock, plunging her head downwards to take me deep into the back of her throat.

She played with my balls as she sucked my cock whilst I moved my face forward and licked her pussy which made her shudder and almost at once Tessa's tangy love juice came flowing out of her cunt and dribbled down my chin.

I clenched my teeth and somehow stopped myself from coming as she looked up at me with shining, moist eyes as she pulled her head away from my cock and threw herself back on the bed.

'Fuck me, Jack, I want to be screwed by your thick Scottish cock, you big-cocked boy!' she panted as I gazed in awe at her hairy quim. She spread her legs and ran her finger between the pink pouting lips of her juicy, dripping honeypot.

'Come on, Jack, I need you,' she panted and I quickly swung myself over the trembling girl and slowly entered her and her tight snatch enveloped my cock like a warm wet glove as my shaft slid between the clinging walls of her love tunnel. Our bodies slid

*against each other as I jerked my hips to and fro as I
fucked her, furiously pistoning my prick in and out of
her creamy cunt at top speed.*

*'I'm coming, Jack, I'm coming!' she cried out
breathlessly. 'Oh God, that's wonderful . . . it's like
fireworks exploding inside my cunt . . . now shoot
your load and we'll make it together!'*

*I paused to catch my breath and then ploughed
on, filling Tessa's tingling crack with the thick tool
she craved for until she screamed with excitement
and bucked her hips in a tremendous convulsive
spasm as she climaxed. This set me off and the
sticky cream burst out of my cock, drenching the
long funnel of her cunt as I rode stiffly in and out of
her cunny until I was milked dry. Then I withdrew
my deflated shaft and rolled off her, my heart
pounding and my chest heaving as I lay gasping
with exhaustion.*

*When I had recovered I sat up and said: 'Hadn't we
better contact Karen and Dave?', but Tessa kissed my
ear and murmured: 'They'll be in room forty seven,
but they probably wouldn't appreciate a call for
another half an hour or so.'*

*Well, as you have probably guessed, Dave and I
never made it to the party for which we had come to
Edinburgh! Tessa managed to get two free seats for
their show at the Assembly Rooms that evening. To be
honest, it was one of those experimental avant-garde
plays and I was so tired from the walk up Arthur's
Seat, carrying down Tessa on my back and of course
the frenetic fuck just before the show that I found it
hard to keep my eyes open, but Dave nudged me in
the ribs when I started to snore! All I can remember is
that Tessa closed the first act by standing alone in the
middle of the stage dressed in a black sweater and*

*tight blue jeans and read out a poem which went
something like:*

> *It was on a winter morn,*
> *And I was reading porn*
> *And I swore*
> *Never to tell.*
> *Well!*
> *I did!*
> *And Johnny Rand looked bland*
> *When they gave him a grand*
> *To pose in a nudie magazine.*
> *Though he wasn't that keen*
> *For he was only sixteen.*

*God knows what that was all about and I wondered
what John Gibson of the* Edinburgh Evening News
*was scribbling on his programme as Tessa walked off
to a lacklustre round of applause.*

*Still, this didn't stop me congratulating the girls on
their performance at the back-stage party afterwards.
Later they smuggled us back into the hotel where the
four of us spent the night fucking and sucking in a
whoresome foursome. But that's another story . . .*

*Write back soon, my bonnie blonde bombshell,
and tell me all your news,*

Love and kisses
Jack

'I'd like to meet Jack Dennison if he ever comes back to
Falmington,' grinned Sharon as she folded up his letter.
'If Belinda would like to make up a threesome, we could
have a lot of fun – which reminds me, where on earth has
she got to? She should have been back by now.'

'Yes, but she didn't want to be seen checking Shane's
booking,' said Denise as she called over the waitress and

ordered an ice-cream for Sharon and a coffee for herself.

'We'll just have to wait,' she added as she settled back in her chair. 'I'm sure she won't be much longer.'

Nevertheless it was almost fifteen minutes later before Belinda returned with a self-satisfied smile on her face. 'Darling, what took you so long?' enquired Sharon as she sat down and slumped into her seat. 'The things I do for you, Sharon Shaw – would you believe that I've just had to fuck Andrew Swaffer to get the information you wanted!'

'Andy Swaffer? The guy that owns the Berkeley?' said Sharon in a shocked voice. 'Christ, how on earth did he come into the picture?'

Belinda puffed out her cheeks and said: 'Well, I found the reservation for "Mr Reynolds" in the register quickly enough. That was no problem, but there were no details of time of arrival or which room he was going to be given. Miss Robson had underlined his name in red ink which meant that the reservation had come through Mr Swaffer's office.

'I had seen him leave the hotel as I came in so I thought that now would be a good time to take a chance and look through his files if I could slip by his secretary. As luck would have it, she wasn't at her desk so I trotted into his private room and soon found a letter from Lennie Lieberman, Shane's manager, confirming the booking of the penthouse suite for Friday and Saturday nights. Shane will be arriving at about half-past ten and as you said, Denise, he'll be using the name Michael Reynolds when he checks in.

'Incidentally, Shane isn't paying the bill himself, all he has to do is sign the account which we then have to send on to Mr Lieberman.'

'That'll be because there are no flies on Lennie,' said Denise, who had recently read about Shane's shrewd mentor in the *Daily Mirror*. 'He'll put down Shane's visit as a tax deduction for research.'

'You reckon? Then perhaps I can do the same for the cost of a new pair of panties,' said Belinda promptly as she brought out a pair of ripped cotton knickers from her skirt pocket. 'Andy Swaffer tore these when he pulled them off.'

Denise frowned and said angrily: 'The rotten so and so! You should make sure that he buys you a new pair. If he won't, then I certainly will.'

'Thanks, love,' said Belinda, gratefully acknowledging the offer with a thumbs-up sign. 'But that won't be necessary. I'm sure that Andy will cough up. He's a randy old sod but he's not mean about fringe benefits.'

'But what happened?' demanded Denise as she signalled a passing waitress and ordered Belinda coffee. 'Did this happen because he caught you looking at his personal papers?'

She answered: 'Not exactly, but he did come in just as I was putting the folder back into the filing cabinet – and naturally he asked me what I was doing in his office. I told him that Lucy, his former secretary, had called and asked if I could send her another copy of the reference Andy had written for her after she had resigned last year.

'He had the grace to blush because Lucy had been forced to leave after a guest complained that one evening, as he was walking through the hotel car park, he had noticed some activity in the back of a Morris Minor. When he had peered through the window, he had seen Lucy bending over some lucky fellow and sucking his naked cock! This so shocked him that he went straight to Freddie Newman, the duty manager, to complain and insisted that Freddie telephoned the police straightaway so that they could come round and arrest the couple concerned.

'The rotten old sod!' exclaimed Sharon warmly. 'Freddie should have told him to eff off – since when is sucking cocks against the law?'

'Sucking off is not against the law although funnily enough it is illegal even in the privacy of your own bedroom in some Southern American states,' said Denise mildly. 'But even in the most civilised countries like Sweden, any sort of fucking is illegal in a public place.

'Well, what did the duty manager do?' she asked and Belinda shrugged and said: 'Fred tried to cool the chap down but when it became clear that he couldn't make this geezer change his mind, he suggested that he took his complaint directly to Mr Swaffer. So the chap marched round to Andy's office and of course, Andy was nowhere to be seen for the simple reason that it was his prick which Lucy had been busy gobbling in the back of her car!

'Anyhow, he must have pulled his trousers up pretty smartish because he turned up a couple of minutes later. He too tried to dissuade his guest from calling the police, but this chap was a lay preacher and insisted that the police were called, especially because he had recognised Lucy as a member of the hotel staff.

'Now I don't altogether blame Andy. He couldn't risk having his name or the Berkeley involved in a sex scandal so when the guy said that he would not ring the police if the girl was instantly dismissed, the poor chap had little choice but to agree.

'So Lucy resigned the morning and I understand that Andy gave her a hundred pounds as a leaving present. We were quite close and we kept in touch for a while after she left Falmington, but I haven't heard from her since last March when she sent me a postcard from Bournemouth to say she had landed a good job at one of the posh hotels there.'

Sharon grunted: 'Huh, at least that story had a happy

ending. Anyhow, what did Andy Swaffer say when you mentioned Lucy's name?'

Belinda winked at her and chuckled: 'Now this is where it all gets rather interesting! He sat down in his chair and then just as I was walking to the door, I heard a loud sneeze come from where Andy was sitting. "What the devil——," I began when I was interrupted by another huge sneeze and who should scramble out stark naked from underneath his desk but young Wendy Sheffield, his pretty new secretary! No wonder she hadn't been at her desk outside Andy's room when I went through into his office! Obviously, she had been expecting him and had dived under the desk when I suddenly appeared out of the blue.

'She must have been about to give her boss a hand job because when he stood up, his zip was undone and there was already a sizeable swelling in the front of his trousers. Now I thought very quickly about that I should do – I reckoned that if I could get him on our side, so to speak, it would make things far easier all round when Shane arrived. It's not as if I were telling him anything he didn't know already about Shane's visit, so I decided to take Wendy's place when she grabbed her dress and fled out of the office, slamming the door behind her.'

There was silence for a moment as Denise and Sharon exchanged glances and then Denise expelled a deep breath and threw out her arms as she exclaimed: 'Well, you're a real star, Belinda! You deserve a medal for fucking beyond the call of duty!'

But Belinda shrugged her shoulders and said: 'Oh, come on, it was nothing special! Actually, I've always fancied Andy Swaffer so I was more than happy to pull him close to me and stick my tongue inside his mouth and slip my hand down and give his prick a nice squeeze.

'This did the trick! Inside a minute Andy had unbuttoned my dress, unhooked my bra and started to nuzzle his lips against my titties – not that I minded as I adore having my nipples nibbled and this was really turning me on. Then I unzipped his trousers and pulled out his big bare cock and dropped to my knees and began tonguing him up and down his veiny truncheon. He heaved and grunted like some old steam engine when I took his uncapped knob into my mouth and started to suck. He shot his load almost at once.'

Sharon let out a low chuckle as she observed: 'So if he came so quickly why were you away for so long?'

'Because by now we both wanted a real fuck,' replied Belinda simply. 'It took a little while for Andy to get hard again but after we had stripped off he went down on me and licked me out beautifully, slipping his tongue inside my juicy crack and playing with my clitty which finished me off almost as quickly as I had brought him off.'

She sat back in her chair and sighed. Little dimples appeared on Belinda's cheeks as her lips broke into a languid, feline smile. Then she continued: 'It didn't take long for me to get Andy's prick up to the mark. I only had to wash over his helmet with my tongue and his shaft was fully erect and as hard as steel. When he was ready, he sat in his big leather chair and I straddled him and slid his cock deep inside my sticky quim, bouncing up and down on his rigid rammer whilst he licked and lapped on my titties.

'We let ourselves go and I really enjoyed myself as Andy jerked his hips upwards in time with my downward thrusts and I came twice before a jet of jism splashed inside my cunny. Oh, there's nothing I like better than a bumpy ride on a rock-hard thick prick and then feel a gush of warm spunk cream my cunt.'

'Even so, you did a grand job, Belinda,' said Denise.

'If there's ever anything I can do for you in return, just let me know.'

Belinda laughed and replied: 'Well, it was fun bonking Andy Swaffer. But fixing it for me to fuck Shane Hammond might not be so easy because, according to that letter from your boss, he's only coming to Falmington to screw this girl called Sandie, whoever she may be.'

'I'd also like to know who she is. It could be useful when I make my pitch for Shane's book,' Denise commented thoughtfully. 'And he probably met her at that party for Shane and the band after the concert at the Berkeley Hotel.'

Denise was quite correct in this assumption. Indeed it was Andy Swaffer himself who had introduced the mysterious Sandie to the world-famous rock star during the party the relieved hotelier had thrown to celebrate the handsome profit he had made in financing Shane Hammond's concert, although he had several sleepless nights when at one stage it appeared that he would fail to gain permission to stage the Sunday night show from the Town council.*

He had been aided and abetted in his efforts to swing the vote by Bernie Gosling, Falmington-On-Sea's hard-working publicity manager. In fact the girl concerned was Bernie's personal assistant, the nubile Sandie Walters.

Shane had been bowled over by the gorgeous girl from the minute he had been introduced to her by Andy Swaffer. There was no doubt that Sandie deserved the sex-kitten label Bernie Gosling had mentally bestowed on her when she had first come into his office to be interviewed for a job. From her Italian grandmother she had inherited seductively high cheekbones and generous red

* See 'Summer School 2: All Night Girls' [New English Library]

lips and Shane was further smitten by her soft auburn hair which tumbled down the sides of her face in the fashionably loose style which Jean Shrimpton and other models had made so popular.

The attraction had been mutual, but they had only the opportunity to talk for five minutes at most before Shane had been hustled away to meet the Mayor of Falmington and other local dignitaries. However, he had scribbled down her phone number and though it was Shane's usual practice not to bother with girls who could not make the well-worn trek to his pad in Chelsea, on this occasion he was happy to travel down to Falmington to see Sandie again.

As it so happened, at the very moment that Denise was wondering about the whereabouts of Shane Hammond's secret new girl friend, Sandie Walters could have been found less than half a mile away in the flat which she had bought with an inheritance from her late Aunt Maud a few weeks after starting work in Bernie Gosling's office.

As Denise was talking, Sandie was soaking herself in a warm bath with her long fingers loitering wickedly around the dark curls between her thighs. She lay back and thought about her coming date with the ruggedly handsome rock idol. Her pulse started to race with excitement and her hand rubbed sensuously along her hairy mound as, not for the first time, Sandie pictured in her mind how at the party Shane was wearing his jeans in the sexiest way she had ever seen, the denim fabric shaping his tight trim buttocks and in front the material bunched up in just the right way to display his bulging crotch.

She threw back her head and closed her eyes, her thighs parting as she felt the inside of her cunny moisten when she moved her fingers down to play with her pussy, stroking gently with a rhythmic delicate touch back and forth along the lips.

'Ohhhh! Ohhhh! Ohhhh!' she moaned softly as a mild ripple passed through her groin. Her fingers began to circle around the tiny swelling bud of her clitty, and then she shuddered with delight at the warm glow which suffused the girl's entire body. She slipped a fingertip inside her juicy cunt, churning it inside her love channel whilst her thumb slowly rubbed over the shaft of her engorged clitty which was growing even larger with the passion of unfulfilled desire.

Now her other hand moved upwards to palm each stiffening tawny nipple in turn, rubbing the rubbery titties between her thumb and index finger as electric currents of sheer delight coursed through her. She rubbed her clitty even more forcefully with her thumb. Within moments, the force of her oncoming orgasm started to rock through her in a tidal wave of ecstatic joy which made her groan and rock her knees back and forth in the water.

Sandie let out a low groan and her hands became still, resting in her cunt as the sweet warmth faded away. Then she pulled out the plug and quickly washed away the sticky cum from her fingers before stepping out of the bath and wrapping herself up in the soft warm folds of a welcoming towel.

Some sixty miles away in Shane Hammond's new luxury maisonette off the King's Road, Chelsea, the rock star had already undressed and was lying naked on his bed as he watched the pretty teenage girl with peroxide blonde hair. He had selected her for a swift coupling out of the gaggle of groupies who regularly camped outside his flat. Now she was starting to unzip her skin-tight black mini-skirt.

'What's your name again, love?' he asked whilst the slim girl unhooked her bra and her firm adolescent breasts jiggled enticingly as she rolled down her panties to reveal a dark thicket of pubic curls.

'Trish,' she replied as she swallowed down the remainder of the large vodka and tonic she had requested when he had offered her a drink. Shane frowned as he laid his head back and let Trish straddle him, her knees on either sides of his thighs.

By now his cock should have been as stiff as a poker yet for some reason even this sexy acquisition in his long line of conquests could raise only a flicker of interest in his groin whilst her cool fingers tenderly caressed his balls. However, the girl hid any disappointment she might have felt as he fondled her hanging breasts. Dipping her tousled head, she kissed his nipples and then left a trail of wet kisses all over his chest and belly until her lips descended down into his curly pubic thatch.

However, his recalcitrant cock still refused to stiffen even when Trish licked all round his shaft, nipping gently with her teeth at the loose, wrinkled foreskin. She kept sucking and licking his meaty tool but his shaft stayed obstinately soft even when she gulped in his prick inside her mouth and pumped her head up and down his barely thickened member.

I hope this doesn't mean another visit to Doctor Yenta, reflected Shane as he closed his eyes and tried imagining how different it would be this coming weekend when he would hopefully be running his hands across the sensuous curves of Sandie Walters. Thoughts of his girlfriend thankfully had some effect and at last his cock began to thicken as Trish slicked her fist up and down the burgeoning fleshy pole and licked his cock, the tip of her wet tongue flickering in the ultra-sensitive area just behind his scrotum.

Then Trish opened her lips wide and somehow managed to stuff his entire ballsack inside her mouth. She grabbed his pulsing stiffstander with both hands and held the purple helmet in front of her face, gazing at it for a moment before she took his balls out of her mouth and started to nibble and suck the length of his thick nine-inch boner.

No, I won't have to visit Doctor Yenta again, thought Shane happily as Trish stroked her tongue along the underside of his cock before gobbling in his helmet between her lips and establishing a sweet rhythm as she bobbed her head up and down, gradually swallowing more and more of his polished veiny pole.

Then Trish changed tack and let go of Shane's throbbing tadger from her mouth, relishing the distinctive salty taste in her mouth of his precum. She prepared to engulf his cock with another similar but subtly different part of her anatomy.

She rose up and mounted him, taking hold of his palpitating prick and fed the hungry maw of her pussy with his cock, sliding his knob between her pussy lips as she ground her hips down, swaying from side to side so that his penis was totally enfolded inside her tingling quim. She rocked herself on his thick prick, lifting herself up until only Shane's knob remained inside her love channel and then dropping down again to bury its glistening length inside her clinging, wet sheath.

The teenage girl rode him like Lester Piggott on the favourite at Goodwood, savagely thrusting herself down upon his trembling tool. Shane soon caught the rhythm and thrust upwards in time with her downward plunges so that his prick rubbed delightfully against her clitty whilst Trish tensed and released the wave-like muscles of her cunt.

Without taking his quivering cock out of her dripping

slit, he rolled the delicious young girl onto her back and began pumping his tingling shaft in and out of Trish's juicy crack, now even more aroused by the thrilling sight of her velvety love lips opening and closing over his gleaming blue-veined truncheon. Their mouths crushed together as she wriggled her backside to absorb every last inch of his shaft as he pushed himself into her until their pubic hairs were matted together and his balls bounced against the soft cheeks of her tight little backside.

'Aaah! Aaah! that's so nice, Shane,' Trish wailed as he slewed his shaft backwards and forwards inside her sopping slit. 'Keep working your big cock in and out of my cunt, Shane! Yes! Yes! Yes!'

The bedsprings groaned as the randy couple fucked away frenetically until she screamed: 'I'm coming! I'm coming! Now spunk into me! That's the way, oooh, what a flood!' Shane shuddered as a gush of sticky jism burst out of his prick and flooded her quim as Trish bucked and twisted her way to her climax.

Well, that shows that I don't need any more help from Doctor Yenta but I have to take a break, thought Shane dizzily as he rolled over onto his back, his chest heaving as he fought to recover his breath. Trish stretched forward and kissed his glistening wet shaft which was no longer stiff but still looked full and heavy as it lay across his thigh.

'Thanks for a great fuck, Trish, hope you enjoyed it as much as me,' he said politely as she snuggled up beside him. 'Help yourself to a drink, love, and let's just rest for a bit. I don't want to sound rude but we'll have to say bye-bye soon because my manager is coming round for a business meeting in about half an hour.'

'That's okay, Shane, I understand,' she said as she looked at her watch. 'Actually, I don't have too much time, I must get back to the hotel pretty sharpish or I'll be late for my shift.'

'Which hotel do you work in?' asked Shane. 'I love hotels, I've found that spending a weekend even here in London where I live is the best way for me to unwind. I get really mellow after a day or two of just lying in bed ordering my meals and generally just messing around.'

Trish gave a tiny grunt as she observed: 'Yeah, I can see that because I work as a chambermaid at the Grand Imperial. Believe me, you get to see it all in plush city hotels. Honestly, you wouldn't credit some of the things you find between the sheets after guests have checked out – used French letters, rolled-up tubes of KY jelly, porno magazines, the lot! And you'd be surprised how often people forget to lock their doors or hang up the 'Do Not Disturb' cards. Crikey, if I had a pound in my purse for every time I've walked in to find a couple humping away, I'd be worth a nice few bob, that's for sure.

'Only the other morning when I was helping out the room service staff, I knocked on the door with breakfast for one of our regulars, a chap who calls himself Roger Tagholm. He visits the hotel at least once a month, but always with a different dollybird who signs in as his wife. There's never any bother because he slips the night manager a fiver now and then, but I've never actually seen him on the job before.'

'Didn't they hear you knock on the door?'

'No, the radio was on and Mr Tagholm was sitting on the bed facing the window with his lips glued to those of this dishy bird, who was on his lap with her legs wrapped around his waist. His hands were busy kneading her bum cheeks whilst she was so busy smearing his shaft with baby oil that she didn't look up to see me standing there.

"Okay, that'll do," she said to him as she ran her hand between her thighs to fondle herself. "Sorry, you've had to wait, Roger, but my pussy's a bit dry this morning and you have such a big dick that I need to be nice and wet before you fuck me. Now just stay still, and let me do the work."

"No matter, Penny, I'd have waited all day for another chance to fuck your lovely tight cunt," he replied as she adjusted her position on his lap.

'Well, what was I supposed to do? I know how gutted I'd feel if somebody had interrupted me right at the beginning of a good fuck, so I just stood there and peered round to see his helmet slide between her pussy lips as she jiggled up and down on his thick shaft which really was one of the biggest I've seen in years, at least ten inches long.

"Ooooh! It's just as well I rubbed in the baby oil," she breathed as the first four or five inches disappeared inside her as she slid her weight down upon his colossal cock. She paused for a moment and then managed to lower herself further, taking in another inch or so of his enormous stiffie.

'Meanwhile, I stood there mesmerised at the sight of Mr Tagholm's huge balls lolling in the vee of his crotch whilst Penny bounced up and down on his rigid veiny pole, sliding up and down in little jerks as she eased yet another inch or two of his gigantic tool inside her on each downstroke.

'It wasn't possible for the girl to cram any more cock inside her cunny – she had only an inch or two to go but now she balanced herself with her spread fingers pressing against his tummy as she wiggled from side to side and then cried out: "Jesus Christ, I've never been so full of cock!"

'Mr Tagholm gripped her side as she slithered up and down his immense truncheon as she rode his cock and then his face contorted with effort as he cried out:

"Yowee! I'm coming, Penny, I can't stop it!"

"It's okay Roger, shoot your load, I'm coming too," she howled and she shivered all over and then slumped down on him, forcing them both back onto the bed where they rolled around cackling with laughter. Believe it or not, I don't think they even noticed me leaving their breakfast tray on the dressing table and walking out of the room. I didn't half feel horny afterwards, I can tell you!'

Shane grinned as he observed: 'I believe you – and I bet you often get the hots for some of the guests anyhow.'

Trish shook her head and commented: 'Not as often as you might think, although last month there was a couple of good-looking young businessmen from Denmark who I fancied. Real Nordic types they were with their short blond hair, long legs and firm little bums. Someone told me that they were in the film business and were here to negotiate some deal with a British distributor. Anyway, they spent a lot of time in meetings in their suite and Harry, the room service waiter, told me they were very polite and always gave him a good tip when he served them with drinks.

'Like most of the Scandinavians I've come across, they were big drinkers and one night, when I had just finished the late shift, they called down for a bottle of champagne. Poor Harry was rushed off his feet so I said I would take it up to them on my way up to bed.

'Well, as soon as Mr Jensen opened the door, I could tell that this wasn't the first bottle he and his friend Mr Borgmann had knocked back that evening! His face was flushed and he welcomed me in like a friend rather than as a waitress. He signed the bill and then gave me a pound note which was the best tip I'd had for some time.

'I thanked him and he said: "Well, if you really want to thank me, you will help me drink this champagne. My name is Bernard, by the way. Erland, my partner, is in the bathroom but I think he has gone to sleep in there as he began celebrating the contract we signed this afternoon a little earlier than me".

'I accepted his offer and we shook hands very formally when I told him my name. Then I asked him what deal he had just concluded. Would you believe, Bernard told me that he and Erland made nudie movies for the Middle East. It appears that the Arabs will pay a fortune to see blonde girls show off their tits and pussies and now they were now teaming up with some people in London to distribute their films in England.

"Whilst we are here we shall make a film in London – tomorrow we'll have to advertise for girls to star in the film. You wouldn't know of any girls who might be interested in appearing in it?"

"It depends what is involved," I replied but he added quickly: "Oh, I promise there is nothing hard-core involved, just tits and bums and simulated sex," he explained as he opened the bottle. "There's a big home movies market now that so many people have projectors for Super-8 film. They won't need any experience, just the ability to act naturally and look sexy when they strip off their clothes. It won't pay badly either, for I told our British associates that we must attract the best girls to earn a good reputation with our potential customers."

"So how much would a girl earn to make one of your films?" I asked and he answered: "Well, we shoot a film in six or seven days and we will pay the actors fifty pounds a day cash."

"Wow, for that sort of money I might be interested myself," I exclaimed and the long and short of it was that by the time we had finished the champagne I agreed to audition for the film. "There's no time like the present," I said, kicking off my shoes and before you could say Jack Robinson I was parading in front of Bernard dressed only in a pair of scanty black knickers.

"So have I passed the test?" I enquired as I gathered up my bare breasts in my hands and squeezed them together as though offering them to Bernard who was sitting on the bed with his trousers tented out by a massive bulge in his lap.

"Absolutely, with flying colours as I think you say," he said hoarsely. I sat down next to him and stroked the length of his erection as I said softly: "Great! Then why don't we rehearse a scene here and now?"

'I didn't have to say any more for Bernard let out a lustful growl and pulled me towards him. We French kissed whilst his hands cupped my bare breasts and then he peeled off my panties before tearing off his own clothes. When we were both naked we lay down together on the bed and my cunt began to moisten as his fingers entwined themselves in my muff. I parted my thighs to let him diddle me and soon he was doing wild things to my clitty which made me come all over his fingers.

'Now just as it happened with Mr Tagholm and his bird, we were threshing around so violently that we didn't hear Erland come in from the bathroom until I saw him standing at the foot of the bed. Now I was too far gone to stop twisting around whilst Bernard was sliding his fingers in and out of my quim. I think the three of us felt the current of sexual energy which was building up – certainly I could see it as I watched Erland's trousers tent outwards as his prick pushed against his trousers.

'I'd never had two men together before and Bernard must have read my mind because he whispered: "Go on, Trish, I've no objections if you want to pull out his cock," I breathed hard, tugged down the zip and fished inside the slit for Erland's rock hard boner. Like Bernard, he was circumcised but his shaft was one of those short, barrel-like tools which always bring me off as the sides slide along my clitty.

'Anyway, he stripped off in double quick time and jumped on the bed to join us and we lay together in a marvellous lovers' sandwich. A shudder passed through me as I felt Bernard's prick slide between my legs, moving neatly back and forth over my excited clitty whilst Erland's cock ran along the crevice between my bum cheeks, hot and throbbing against my cool skin.

'We moved in unison and my fingers circled Erland's balls as I rolled over and knelt over Bernard, kissing his smooth wide knob whilst Erland moved round and slid his face under my bottom and swirled his tongue deep inside me as he sucked on my cunny lips. Then he pushed two fingers inside me and started to massage the sensitive inner walls of my cunt. As his mouth closed over my clitty, I pushed myself against his face and came, flooding his face with my love juice as I gobbled in Bernard's shaft down my throat.'

She paused and Shane said lightly: 'Was his cock as tasty as one of Grodzinski's Danish pastries?' and this made her giggle as she replied: 'It sure did, but he didn't come in my mouth. Instead, he said something in Danish to Erland whilst he pulled his shaft away and rolled over to my right side, and then he began stroking his tool and rubbing the helmet against my erect nipple. Erland then moved to my other side and directed his knob against my left tit to do the same. I found it so exciting watching these two guys wank themselves off on my boobs that my hand shot down between my legs and I started to finger-fuck myself, bringing myself off again and again.'

'Then I suppose they fucked you,' remarked Shane, but Trish shook her head and said: 'I wouldn't have minded but right then the telephone rang and Erland had to get dressed and meet somebody on business downstairs. Still, I got up on my knees and Bernard fucked me very nicely doggie-style so all was not lost.'

'And are you going to make the movie for these characters?' asked Shane and Trish smiled happily and said: 'Yup, I've signed a contract and we're going to start filming down in some little seaside resort on the Sussex coast next weekend.'

For God's sake, it would be too much of a coincidence, groaned Shane to himself but sure enough she went on blithely: 'Yes, we're staying at a posh hotel called the Berkeley in somewhere called Falmington-On-Sea. Hey, didn't I read in the *Melody Maker* that you played a gig there a couple of weeks ago?'

'That's right, it's a quiet little place and I'm sure you'll have fun there,' said Shane with a heavy heart. The last thing he wanted was for any groupie to grab hold of him whilst he was with Sandie Walters. Nevertheless he wished her luck before he continued: 'Look, I don't want to chuck you out but we've both got work to do this evening so I think you'd better start making a move.'

'Yup, I'll get dressed and be on my way,' agreed Trish as she swung herself out of bed and bent down and picked up her knickers. 'The boys have promised me a copy of the film when it's finished and I'll come round and show it to you.'

'Yes, you do that, love,' he murmured as, impatient for her to leave, he hauled himself out of bed and slipped on a blue silk dressing gown. Thankfully, Trish was a quick dresser and walked out into the street more than happy with a signed copy of Shane's new LP whilst the rock star walked into the bathroom and switched on the shower.

Chapter Three

Going For A Take

Kneeling on their bed between Sharon's parted thighs, Denise surveyed the fluffy bush of blonde hair which lightly covered the younger girl's pubic mound. It took only seconds for her to decide that this was where she wanted to go. On her hands and knees she bent forward to kiss her there, causing a shiver to run up Sharon's spine.

'My, my, you're very wet this morning,' said Denise in a muffled voice as she licked along the length of Sharon's moistening crack. 'I can guess what you've been dreaming about, you naughty puss!'

'Ha, ha, very funny, although you wouldn't be entirely wrong,' replied Sharon drowsily. 'It was a funny old dream at that – Sir Stafford Stiffkey was showing me around Parliament and when we were in the actual chamber of the House of Commons, he sat down on one of the front benches and told me to take off all my clothes.'

Denise lifted her mouth from Sharon's cunny and stared up at her with an amused expression on her face as she queried: 'What, in front of all those MPs? Well, I suppose that's probably a better way than most to attract the attention of the Speaker!'

Sharon let out a sleepy chuckle and answered: 'Maybe,

but it was lucky that the chamber was empty or Sir Stafford would have been escorted out by the Sergeant-at-Arms or whatever they call him. Because whilst I was undressing, he suddenly ripped open his trousers and brought out this immense throbbing shaft. This prick really puzzled me when I dropped to my knees to take a closer look after he asked me to suck him off.'

'I don't see what's so strange about that,' observed Denise as her fingertips toyed with the teenage girl's pouting pussy lips. 'After all, what did you expect him to do – give you a camera and ask you to take a photograph of his hard-on?'

'No, not really. What I couldn't understand was that I had to jam down his foreskin when I grabbed hold of his tool although I'm almost certain that Sir Stafford's cock is circumcised,' she replied. Before Denise could question her further, she explained how she had caught sight of their local M.P.'s wedding tackle when on her errand to pick up some papers for Bruce Teplin from him.

'I didn't let him fuck me, you know,' said Sharon with a touch of indignation. She had seen a smile forming on Denise's lips.

'Of course you didn't,' agreed Denise as she nibbled on the blonde girl's nut hard little clitty which made Sharon wriggle as she complained: 'Oooh, stop doing that or I won't be able to tell you the rest of my dream! Well, I unhooked my bra and, cupping my hands under my breasts, I rubbed my titties along Sir Stafford's shaft and then trapped it between my boobs. Then I bent my head and began to give Falmington-On-Sea's M.P. a blow job, gulping his knob into my mouth whilst I reached down and slid a finger into my wet pussy.

'I was beginning to enjoy myself but just as I washed his helmet with my tongue, who should come striding in but George Brown!'

'What, the Foreign Secretary?' exclaimed Denise and Sharon nodded and went on: 'That's the man! He stood over me, swaying slightly as if he'd knocked back a drink or two and then he unzipped his flies as he barked out: "Comrade Shaw, what are you doing licking a Tory's tadger? What's wrong with a good stiff Labour organ?"

"I'm not a member of your party, Mr Brown," I said as I clasped hold of his thick pulsing pole. "I'm not even old enough to vote and even if I were, I wouldn't give it to you or to Sir Stafford's lot. My family have always voted for the Liberals."

"No problem then! You can suck us both off because you wouldn't want to show favour to the Right or to the Left," said the Foreign Secretary as he pushed his thick tool towards my lips. I found myself gobbling both him and Sir Stafford, licking one tool and then the other. My pussy was really starting to tingle with excitement when I woke up and found your head between my legs!

'I wonder what it all means,' she sighed and Denise shrugged her shoulders and kissed her pungent pussy. 'Perhaps you should join the Beatles and trek off to the Himalayas to ask the Maharashi Mahesh Yogi,' she suggested. She moved her index finger slowly into Sharon's sopping cunt. 'Your hero John Lennon seems to believe that the Yogi knows the answer to almost everything. In the meantime, I fancy a nice drink of cunny juice, so why don't you just lie back and let me finish you off.'

Sharon gurgled with appreciation as Denise's wicked tongue dipped into the crevice of her pink folds, poking between the love lips and running it up and down the slippery grooves. She was so wet that Denise had to gulp down a mouthful of cuntal juice. Thrusting her tongue in and out of Sharon's cunt, Denise lapped up the tangy syrup of the girl's fast approaching orgasm.

'Oh God, I'm coming,' Sharon panted when she felt Denise's tongue rake over her erect clitty which had popped out of its pod. Sharon wrapped her thighs around Denise's head as she sought to open herself more to her lover's questing tongue.

Denise slid her hands underneath her to clasp the soft fleshy globes of her bum cheeks as she switched her attention to Sharon's clitty, lightly scraping her teeth along the nub which finally sent the girl over the edge and brought a fresh flood of tangy love juice into Denise's mouth. Sharon trembled all over as the overwhelming rush of passion swept over her.

'There's no time for any more fucking, more's the pity,' said Denise reluctantly as she swung herself off the bed and padded into the bathroom. 'Would you like to have a go at finishing that crossword in last night's paper whilst I take the first bath?'

'Sure thing,' said Sharon absently. When Denise returned, she was greeted by Sharon waving a copy of the *Falmington Telegraph* at her.

'Did you finish the crossword then?' she asked but Sharon ignored the question with a dismissive wave of her hand. 'Sod the bloody crossword, darling, just look at this advert on page three,' she replied as she thrust the newspaper in front of Denise's face. 'See, I've ringed it: "Bright young men and women required by Continental film-maker for scenes to be shot this coming weekend in Falmington. Fifty pounds cash per day. For further information, phone Mr Jensen, Falmington 6000 after eleven o'clock on Friday morning." That's the Berkeley Hotel's number – I'll give this Mr Jensen a ring from Bruce's office at the College.

'Do you fancy having a go? We haven't got much on this weekend and I wouldn't mind the chance of earning some cash in hand.'

'Well, you might not be too busy this weekend, but haven't you forgotten that the one and only Shane Hammond's arriving at the Berkeley this evening?' complained Denise as she smacked the excited girl on the shoulder with the paper. 'Remember, Belinda told us that he's not expected in till about half past ten tonight, but I'll be there from nine thirty just to make sure I don't miss him. Then I'll probably be camped in the hotel for the duration. With any luck I'll be tied up with Shane all over the weekend!

'But you go ahead and see what's being offered,' she added as she kissed Sharon on the lips and squeezed her firm young breasts. 'With your looks, sweetie, I'll bet this guy signs you up on the spot and you'll be on your way to Hollywood within the month!'

Denise was working at home that morning and Sharon left the flat at a reasonable time to get to work, but her bus broke down less than a minute after she had boarded it and Bruce Teplin was already at his desk when she finally arrived at the College.

To Sharon's surprise, the usually testy lecturer did not carry out his threat to report her unpunctuality to the personnel department – indeed, to her relief, he accepted her explanation about the problem with her bus without as much as a murmur.

Of course, what Sharon did not know was that the wheel of fortune had rolled in Bruce Teplin's direction the previous evening. Rosie O'Hara had already informed him that she would be in Birmingham over the weekend at a conference, though this would have upset him less if she had not also told him that he could not fuck her again until her specialist had checked that all was well with her diaphragm.

However, less than ten minutes later his girl friend,

Katie Summerfield, had telephoned him with the news that Doctor Yenta had suddenly been called away earlier that day to treat a member of the Royal Family.

'It's all so terribly hush hush that I don't even know where he's gone, let alone who he's actually treating,' she had said gleefully. 'Anyhow, I've had to cancel all his Friday appointments and he gave me the day off so I thought I'd come down to Falmington over the weekend. Your landlady won't mind if I stay with you for a couple of nights, will she?'

Katie had discovered that a mutual friend was driving to the coast on business, leaving London early on Friday morning. He would be happy to give her a lift to Falmington which was only a few miles out of his way. She had gone on: 'I'd best meet you at the College as I'll probably be in Falmington by about noon,' she explained. 'You might remember that Paul Moser drives like the clappers.'

So Bruce Teplin had a smile on his face as he sat down to work. He was eagerly looking forward to seeing Katie Summerfield again, especially as the raunchy nurse had also warned Bruce that, except for the brief encounter with Shane Hammond in Harley Street, she had not had any sex since they had last seen each other. Now she could hardly wait to jump into bed with him.

Mrs Highgate, his landlady, had no objection to Katie sharing his room and as he had no lectures to deliver that day, Bruce planned to clear his desk and take Katie back to his digs as soon as she turned up at the College.

In fact, Katie arrived somewhat earlier than he expected, and it was only half past eleven when Sharon walked down to the reception desk in order to escort her to Bruce Teplin's office. Although Bruce Teplin had not told her that Katie was his girl-friend, Sharon remembered that the girl who had written about screwing Shane

Hammond in a doctor's surgery was from a girl named Katie. And in any case, Bruce had given the game away when he had asked her to book a taxi to take Miss Summerfield and himself back to his lodgings as soon as his visitor arrived.

Sharon could hardly wait to see what Katie was like in the flesh. Although not jealous, for she had no designs whatsoever upon Bruce Teplin, she was surprised that the lecturer had such an attractive girl in tow.

Shane Hammond had fallen for her charms and, out of her uniform, Katie Summerfield was even more of a head-turner as she sat demurely in one of the comfortable leather-backed chairs. If anything, she looked younger than her age of twenty-three for Katie was fresh faced with large liquid hazel eyes, a well shaped nose and a wide, full mouth. This was capped by a mane of glossy auburn hair which she wore in a fringe over her forehead and in long, sleek strands over her ears and down over her shoulders.

She was wearing a low-cut baby blue sweater which showed her firm jutting breasts to good advantage and Sharon doubted whether she was wearing any bra underneath. A good figure too, she noted as she glanced at Katie's crossed legs and the expanse of shapely flesh exposed where her white mini-skirt had ridden up over her thighs.

'Hello Miss Summerfield, I'm Sharon, Dr Teplin's secretary,' said Sharon and the older girl smiled and replied: 'Oh, please call me Katie! Only my dentist and bank manager call me Miss Summerfield! It's nice to meet you, Sharon, and I hope you haven't found Bruce too much of a pain. I'm very fond of him, for he's a totally different person out of the office, but I'm really worried that he's turning into a workaholic hermit.'

There's little danger of that, unless Rosie O'Hara

suddenly loses interest in him, thought Sharon who naturally kept her silence and simply returned Katie's smile as she escorted her up the short flight of stairs.

Sharon was not the only reader whose eye had been caught by the display advertisement in the *Falmington Telegraph*. Belinda Blisswood had taken the opportunity of staying the night with Pierre Truchet at his flat as neither of them had to make an early start the next morning. On the previous evening, Marc Ribeaux had left Falmington with a small group of students for a three day visit to London.

Pierre was fast asleep when Belinda woke up and being a considerate kind of person, rather than disturb her lover, she slipped out of bed to make up a cup of tea and idly scanned the newspaper whilst she waited for the kettle to boil. I must pop in and see this Mr Jensen when I go in to work this afternoon, she thought to herself when she saw the advertisement. Fifty pounds would come in very handy if she decided to take up Pierre's invitation to visit him in France at the end of his summer school course.

She put the newspaper on the tray with two mugs of tea which she carried into the bedroom and placed on the dressing table. During the hot weather, they both slept in the nude and Belinda's eyes twinkled when she lifted a corner of the duvet to see that Pierre's prick was standing stiffly to attention between his thighs. He had one hand on his balls as he lay on his back still deep in slumber.

'I hope you are dreaming about me,' Belinda murmured, gently moving his hand to one side. She bent down and kissed the wide pink dome of his swollen circumcised stiffie and Pierre grunted and muttered some unintelligible words in French into the pillow.

'Come on, Pierre, my pussy is waiting for that thick

shaft of yours,' the lusty young blonde urged him as she slid her fingers around his throbbing truncheon and began to fist her hand up and down his tumescent tadger, rubbing it up to an even greater height. Then Belinda leaned forward and, licking her lips, she took the smooth-skinned dome inside her mouth, her moist lips straining to encircle it as she bobbed her head to and fro, sliding her lips juicily all along the shaft of his quivering cock as her head bobbed up and down until she had taken his full length deep into her throat.

'Urrgh!' gasped Pierre as his eyes snapped open and he looked down at Belinda's tousled mop of hair moving rhythmically between his thighs whilst she rubbed her stalky nipples against his groin. Pierre grinned as he swiftly came to his senses and he murmured: 'Belinda, *ma cherie*, if there were more girls like you, the makers of alarm clocks would soon find themselves out of business!'

The Frenchman groaned as Belinda washed his bulbous bell-end all over with her impish pink tongue before drawing the warm fleshy lollipop deep into the back of her throat as she started to suck vigorously on his palpitating pole. In seconds, Pierre's body began to jerk and then he came in a rush with jets of jism spouting out of his twitching tool. Belinda gulped it down as she milked his cock dry and his shaft began to deflate in her hand.

'My turn now, I think,' said Belinda as she slid back into bed. Pierre kissed the creamy-soft skin of her slightly rounded tummy, pushing his tongue into her belly-button as he moved his head down to begin licking and lapping at her tasty wet pussy.

Without taking his face away from her cunt, Pierre moved right round to lie on his belly between Belinda's thighs. He grunted with satisfaction when he heard her high-pitched squeak as the tip of his tongue slid easily into the red chink between her rolled love lips. However, he did not want to bring the sexy girl to the boil too quickly for his cock needed time to recover its strength from Belinda's delicious blow job. Pierre was careful to avoid the hard nub of her clitty as he licked the walls of her love channel and inhaled the musky cuntal aroma.

Belinda wriggled sensuously and panted out her pleasure as he drew back his head and worked his way upwards, making a trail of kisses until he came to her breasts. He licked each engorged tawny tittie in turn, his lips switching erotically from one erect rubbery nipple to the other.

Then he whispered: 'Turn over,' and when she did the girl sighed with delight as she felt his tongue brushing her back with wide wet strokes until it reached her bum cheeks which he parted with his hands and then his tongue was inside the cleft, exploring, tickling, tasting down towards her cunt and then up again into her arsehole. Belinda shuddered and a rivulet of love juice trickled down her thigh.

In a very short time Pierre's prick began to thicken. He moved his head down again and pushing his head between her wide stretched thighs, his tongue sought out the secrets of her juicy honeypot. The tangy love liquid flowed over his face and her erect little clitty popped out of its shell whilst he nibbled the vibrating love button.

Now that his cock was again as hard as a rock, Pierre pulled her back onto her belly so that he was presented with the sight of her thrillingly dimpled bum cheeks. Belinda was now more than ready to be fucked and, pushing out her delicious young backside, she turned her head to see Pierre position himself behind her. She reached back to slide her fingers around his pulsing prick and placed his knob neatly in the cleft between her pert, rounded buttocks.

Pierre drove home his throbbing cock doggie-style into her welcoming wet cunt and Belinda's bottom responded to his shoves, his balls banging against her smooth bum whilst he jerked his hips to and fro.

'Woooh! That's the way, cork me with your thick prick, you randy fuckpot!' yelled out Belinda uninhibitedly. Pierre snaked his sinewy shaft in and out of her juicy cunt in a steady, shunting motion. He slid his right hand across her tummy and into her fluffy bush to massage her clitty on every forward stroke whilst she rocked and bucked to his rhythm.

They fucked happily away until Belinda was suddenly overwhelmed by the force of a swiftly approaching climax. She screamed out: 'Squirt out your spunk, I'm coming!' and she shivered all over as the orgasm swept through her. Pierre bellowed hoarsely as he shot his load, sending a stream of sticky white seed into her sopping cunny. The randy pair grunted and groaned until the sweet passion finally died away and they lay still on the newly washed white sheet which Pierre noticed was now stained with their juices.

'I'll have to change the bed before Mrs Green comes in this afternoon, we only pay her to do the cleaning and ironing,' he mumbled but Belinda ruffled his hair and said: 'Oh, don't be embarrassed, I'm sure she knows that you don't sleep alone. In fact, it's best if she does know that I often stay overnight or she'll think you spend all your time pulling your pud!

'Playing with yourself,' she added when she saw the blank expression on his face and Pierre chuckled: 'I don't have the strength after a night with you, Belinda. You know, it's exactly four weeks since we started going out together. I should really take you out somewhere like Leon's, that expensive new Spanish restaurant in Humphries Street but as my tutor Dr Teplin would say, I have a cash flow crisis until my parents' cheque arrives next week.'

'Hey, that reminds me of something,' exclaimed Belinda as she swung herself out of her bed and padded across to the dressing table and brought over the *Falmington Telegraph* to Pierre. 'The tea's cold, I'm afraid, I'll make some more after we've got up. Meanwhile, just look at this advert. If we were chosen to appear in the film, you could take me to Leon's for a slap-up meal and I could spend a week in France with you when you go back home.'

'M'mm, it sounds too good to be true. I wonder, how do you say it, if there is a catch?' questioned Pierre as he studied the text. 'Still, I suppose there can be no harm in finding out more information. Isn't Falmington 6000 the telephone number of the Berkeley?'

'It sure is, and I'll find out more from this Mr Jensen as soon as I get to work this afternoon,' said Belinda as she slipped back into bed. 'Now to more immediate matters – I loved that doggie-style fuck, Pierre. What are the chances of my getting your cock nice and stiff again so that we can have another go?'

Katie Summerfield looked around the clean but somewhat faded bedroom which Bruce Teplin had rented for his six-week summer semester as lecturer in business management at the Falmington College of Higher Education.

'Well, it's hardly the Ritz, is it?' she commented as she opened the small suitcase for her weekend stay. 'Not that I should grumble, you know. The lease expired two weeks ago on that little flat I was renting in Hampstead and I've had to move out. My cousin Joanna has found another super place in Belsize Park which we could share, but we can't move in till September. Luckily, another good friend of mine, Marlene – you've met her, Bruce, a tall girl, not that pretty but with a fantastic figure who works as a showroom model for Segal Textiles – is letting me stay with her which is very kind of her but it's hardly ideal.'

'A bit cramped is it?' asked Bruce sympathetically and Katie grunted: 'You could say that. We share a bedroom and whilst that isn't so bad in itself, right now Marlene is being screwed by a hunky young copper from the local nick who came round here when the flat upstairs was burgled recently. Donald (or Donkey Don as I call him) isn't the brightest guy I've ever met by any means, but he's a lovely thick prick which never seems to go limp. Honestly, Bruce, all this week the pair of them have been rutting away all night. And whilst Marlene's enjoying herself I'm lying under the sheets with my fingers in my ears!

'I can't blame her though. The other night I looked across and saw her giving him a wonderfully slurpy blow job. I felt myself get really wet as I watched her suck his cock and saw Donald let fly. So much spunk spouted out of his knob that Marlene couldn't swallow it all and some of his jism dripped down onto her tits. Then he turned her over and, after smearing some Stork margarine on his shaft, he flipped her over and bum-fucked her.'

Bruce's tool stirred as Katie related this anecdote which in fact was a somewhat exaggerated account of what actually took place. But Katie knew how easily Bruce was turned on by listening to her relate a sexy story and she smiled as Bruce said hoarsely: 'I'll bet you were tempted to join in the fun and games.'

'Sure I was,' she admitted, sensuously passing the tip of her tongue across her top lip. 'But with great self-control I just turned over and with great difficulty closed my eyes and went to sleep. Don't you think I deserve a reward for being such a good girl?'

'You certainly do,' he agreed. As she lifted her face upwards, he bent down to kiss her. In a flash Katie's mouth opened and her tongue was lashed around his gums whilst they hugged each other tightly. Seconds later they were entwined in an ardent hug on his bed. Bruce's pulsing stiffstander tented against his trousers as he felt the sensuous warmth of her ripe curves through the soft material of her sweater. He caught his breath when he slid his hands underneath the garment and discovered that she was wearing no bra. He pushed the sweater up to her chin as he moulded her firm rounded breasts in his hands.

'Let's undress, Brucie, it's always nicer to fuck naked,' she whispered in his ear. 'And anyway, I don't want to crease my new skirt!'

He nodded silently and they swiftly threw off their clothes before diving back into their impassioned embrace. Katie squeezed his pulsating prick, running her fingers along the shaft and rubbing the warm, velvet skin before teasing the uncapped helmet with the tip of her tongue. With a low growl, Bruce thrust his shaft deeper inside her mouth and Katie bobbed her head up and down, feeling his wiry pubic curls tickle her nose as she inhaled his musky masculine odour.

She slurped noisily on his quivering tadger whilst Bruce's index finger probed around her moist folds until it found the juicy opening of her cunt.

'My God, you're so *wet*!' he breathed as Katie humped her mound against his hand. Then, pulling his tool out of her mouth, she transferred her lips to his face and muttered: 'Yes, darling, I'm all wet and ready for you to fuck me nice and hard with your lovely thick prick.'

Bruce moved quickly, sliding himself on top of the

trembling girl and pulled apart her pouting pussy lips which were already glistening with anticipatory lust. He balanced himself on top of her as she grasped his tool and guided his knob into the entrance of her clinging love tunnel.

'M'mm, you're so *big*!' Katie panted as she hoisted her hips upwards to greet his wide-domed helmet. 'I feel so filled up.'

At that point he pressed forward with five and then six inches inside her. By the time he had inserted the seventh inch of his swollen shaft, she had wrapped her arms around his body and clamped her feet round his back. Bruce pulled out and re-entered her sopping quim again and again, thrusting as deeply as he could into her clinging crack and Katie's slick cunny clasped his shaft with each long, slow stroke. And then he stayed still, his cock embedded in her pleasure palace, savouring to the full the delicious cuntal contractions as her pussy feasted upon the palpitating pole trapped inside her tingling snatch.

Then they began to move together and Bruce glided his shaft in and out of her juicy cunt in a deceptively slow, lazy rhythm, but sliding deeper and deeper into her slit with every pistoning plunge. Then he raised the tempo and as their lips meshed together Katie raised her buttocks from the bed as he thrust forward, wildly bucking and pushing up to greet him, rubbing her clitty against his cock as he drove in and out of her. Her tingling love funnel clutched at his sliding shaft as he pounded away, rocking himself into her with such force that the bed-springs groaned underneath them.

The wetness was now pouring out from her as they entered the last lap of the race. Their movements quickened and Katie's cunny muscles squeezed so hard around his rigid rod that Bruce could no longer hold back.

'I'm coming, Katie, here it is, take it now, take it!' he rasped, pressing himself in to the hilt and holding tight to her hips to ensure that his greasy cock didn't slip out of Katie's pussy as he shot a tremendous spurt of creamy white seed inside her. The girl purred with pleasure at this grand shafting.

When they had calmed down, Katie leaned over and pulled out a piece of paper from her handbag which she handed to him as she said: 'Bruce, take a look at this advertisement which I tore out of the local newspaper whilst I was waiting for you this morning. I'll bet a pound to a penny that's Bernard Jensen of X-Ray Movies of Copenhagen. I've heard he's looking for pretty girls and handsome guys to appear in his film.'

'And who's Bernard Jensen when he's at home?' enquired Bruce as he read through the advertisement. 'You've never mentioned him to me.'

'I've never actually met him,' admitted Katie. 'But he was pointed out to Joanna at a party only last week. He makes sexy movies for the Arab market – they go bananas for Scandinavian blondes out there, of course – and now he and his partner are setting up a British company to distribute his films in Britain and the Continent.'

'It's probably the same man,' said Bruce carelessly. 'But so what?'

'Now you must promise to keep this under your hat,' said Katie. Although they were quite alone, she glanced round to make sure that they could not be heard. 'But the fact is that Mr Jensen raised the loot for his new British operation from a syndicate run by a West End rag trade magnate named Alan Gottlieb. There's nothing illegal about what the syndicate does, it's simply run like a private merchant bank, but I daresay that the investors would rather not be involved with the businesses in which

Mr Gottlieb invests on their behalf. Doctor Yenta's a member and come to think of it, so is the local MP from down here.'

Bruce Teplin could hardly believe this news. 'Good grief, so you mean Sir Stafford Stiffkey?' he said incredulously. 'Why, the bloody old hypocrite! Only the other day I heard him on the radio making a speech about the need for the Government to clean up TV!'

Katie laughed as she deftly ran her varnished fingernails through his spring mat of chest hair. 'Well, that's as maybe, darling. Nevertheless, you can take it from me that Sir Stafford's a randy old goat. It so happens that he's a close friend of Doctor Yenta and a couple of weeks ago I heard him say how lucky he was not to have caught crabs after a weekend orgy at some high-class tart's country house.'

'The silly beggar had better watch it,' commented Bruce as he lay back and let Katie graze her nails lightly across his chest. 'If the Sunday papers ever catch up with him, it'll be all up with Sir Stafford. He's only got a small majority and if he falls foul of the local pillars of the community, he'll be done for at the next Election.

'Anyhow, let's come back to this Danish gentleman, Mr Jensen. What was so interesting in his advertisement that you tore it out of the paper? Don't tell me that you want to star in a sex film!'

Katie did not answer but slowly lowered her face to his chest so that her loosened glossy hair brushed against his bare skin. Her abundant creamy breasts pressed warm and heavy against his belly, dangerously close to his groin where his penis was already beginning to stir.

'I suppose I must be an exhibitionist at heart because, to be frank, it wouldn't bother me that much,' she murmured as her fingers curled round his thickening tool. 'But I've brought my new camera down with me and I'd be more interested in taking some still photographs whilst Bernie Jensen is filming some scenes in Falmington.'

This surprising information shocked Bruce Teplin and he asked: 'I don't understand, Katie. What on earth would you do with them?'

'Sell them, of course,' she replied promptly as she ran her fist up and down his now fully erect swollen shaft, delighting in the way Bruce's tool twitched under her touch as if pulses of electricity were passing through it. 'You know I've always been keen on photography. Well, one of Joanna's current boy friends is a professional photographer and there's big money in glamour work. He makes at least a hundred pounds a week from sending sets of nudie colour transparencies to American publishers.

'Believe me, Bruce, there are enough girls who would be happy to pose for me, especially as these magazines aren't sold over here. Mind you, there are also some new men's mags coming out in Britain as well and they're already looking for new talent. I might have to negotiate a fee with Bernie to take my pictures, though I'm sure that he could always do with some publicity stills. I might even be able to wangle myself on the set in exchange for a few prints.

'Will you help me, Bruce? This could be a wonderful opportunity to earn some serious money.'

Although he had planned a Saturday visit to the annual Falmington arts and crafts fair organised by Lady Carolyn Caughey in the grounds of her large estate on the outskirts of the town, the thought of watching a blue film being shot was of more appeal than his original idea of strolling round an exhibition of work by local amateur artists.

'Well, I'll help you if I can,' said Bruce with a small smile. 'Though I'm a pretty rotten photographer – all my shots are either out of focus or I put my thumb over the lens!'

Katie grinned as she bent her head down and kissed the smooth dome of his uncapped helmet. 'Leave the photography to me,' she replied as she rubbed his bursting prick. 'Let me just put Percy out of his misery and then I'll contact Bernie Jensen. If I can interest him in the idea, I'll need to write out a model release form. When you go back to your office, perhaps you could get your secretary to type it out and make a dozen copies.

'Still, first things first,' she added huskily as she pumped her hand up and down the straining girth of Bruce's shaft. Then Katie lowered her head and closed her lips around his knob, fluttering her tongue against the warm, twitching flesh. Bruce shuddered from the sensations as she took a deep breath and tightening her lips around his member, she plunged him deep into the back of her throat.

To Katie's delight Bruce's cock grew even thicker and harder in her mouth as he jerked his hips upwards. She slid a hand underneath his buttocks and, matching her movements to his as she bobbed her head up and down his throbbing tool, she suddenly jammed a finger into his bottom.

'Aaagh!' Bruce gasped at the unexpected sensation which jolted through his body. But when she rotated her finger inside the tight channel, he grunted and almost at once spurted a thick gush of jism into her mouth. Katie gulped down his sticky tribute as she removed her finger from his anus and licked him clean with her tongue.

As Katie had forecast, Bernard Jensen listened carefully to her proposal when she telephoned him and invited her to meet him in his room at the Berkeley Hotel later that afternoon. Everything was falling into place so well for the Dane that he could hardly believe his luck. The telephone had hardly stopped ringing with would-be actors of both sexes wanting to audition. Only a handful of them had been put off when he had warned that in the film there was a wild party scene in which some people would be semi-nude – although he had only skated lightly around the subject of participation in the orgy although Trish, Shane Hammond's wham-bam groupie had bowed out.

In his experience, once the extras were on the set, after a few drinks it only needed one or two of his professional 'stars' to start the ball rolling. Bernard had not brought over any of his usual actresses from Copenhagen, but his new British associates had provided excellent replacements in Christine and Mandy, two ravishing strippers from a top Soho night club together with the club's awesomely hung West Indian bouncer who were scheduled to arrive at around nine o'clock tomorrow morning.

Bernard was a qualified film technician and had already set up the camera and sound equipment in the quietly situated bungalow off the Southwick Road which X-Ray Movies had rented for the weekend from none other than Sir Stafford Stiffkey. To be fair, this rental had been arranged through an estate agent and Sir Stafford had no knowledge of Bernard's presence at the Berkeley nor of the use to which the bungalow was about to be put. He had inherited the property some ten years back after the death of an old maiden aunt and though it lay empty for much of the year, the M.P. had not put it on the market. Indeed, he occasionally used it himself as a love-nest at times when it was inappropriate to bed his girl-friend at Austin Manor, his luxurious home in Falmington.

There was a knock on the door and Bernard checked the sheet of paper upon which he had written his appointments – it was half past twelve and so this would be

Belinda Blisswood, the sexy voiced girl who had said she worked at the hotel and so could be available at five minutes' notice. If this girl were half as pretty as she sounded on the telephone, I'll sign her up for a speaking role, thought Bernard as he called out for his visitor to come in.

He was not to be disappointed when the door opened and Belinda swept into the room. Bernard raised his eyebrows as he stared at the nubile blonde who had stood before him in her figure-hugging hotel black minidress which appeared to have been tailored to reduce grown men to tears. Belinda wore her gleaming blonde hair down the sides of her high-cheekboned face and her sparkling blue eyes alone were enough to send Bernard's pulse racing, even though in his work he was often surrounded by a bevy of beautiful naked girls cavorting around him in the studio.

'Miss Belinda Blisswood, I presume?' said Bernard as he rose from his chair. His gaze swivelled down her body from the swelling mounds of her prominent breasts which thrust firmly through the flimsy white material of her blouse to her long legs which were encased in sheer dark stockings.

'Do sit down – can I get you a drink?' he asked, motioning her towards the small settee upon which she sat down and crossed her shapely legs. Her short skirt was now riding up her thighs.

'No thank you, I can't stay very long as I should really be at work,' she replied with a dazzling smile. 'My friend Estelle is covering for me so I must get back as soon as possible.'

'I quite understand,' nodded Bernard as he slipped a fresh piece of paper into his clipboard and pulled his chair up to face her as he continued: 'Well, let's not waste any time. Have you ever performed on the stage?'

'Not professionally,' she admitted. 'Although I acted in the school play when I was in the sixth form. I played Mistress Quickly in *Henry the Fifth*. That's by Shakespeare, you know.'

Bernard allowed himself a ghost of a smile. 'Yes, I studied English Literature for my degree back in Denmark so I am familiar with the play. But I can't see a glamorous girl like you playing a blowsy old innkeeper like Mistress Quickly.'

'Ah, but you see I played the part more as a barmaid,' explained Belinda, graciously inclining her head as she acknowledged his compliment. 'And I think I was rather good as I was given a super review by Alun Owen, the drama critic of the local newspaper. Mind you, I would have to have been really awful not to have had a good review because Mr Owen's a professional artist and when I was sixteen I earned some extra pocket money by posing for him in the nude.'

'Your parents didn't mind?' queried Bernard and Belinda treated him to a second sparkling smile. 'To be honest, they didn't know. My dad might have blown his top but I don't think Mum would have minded too much – she's much more broad-minded.

'Anyhow, nothing took place between us that I didn't want to happen,' she added enigmatically which made Bernard chuckle as he went on: 'Well, so long as you're eighteen, your parents don't have to know about the film either. May I take it that you'd have no objection in taking part in the nude orgy scene I mentioned on the telephone?'

She thought for a moment and said with a shrug: 'I don't mind so long as any fellas involved don't get too carried away and start taking liberties. It's not that I'll mind any of them waving an erect cock at me, but to be blunt they had better remember that the orgy's not for real or they'll be liable to get a swift knee in the nuts!'

'Quite so,' agreed Bernard sympathetically. 'Belinda, may I asked if you have a boy friend who might be interested in taking part? After all, it would make life far easier all round to have a partner of your choice in the orgy scene.'

'Oh yes, I was going to tell you that Pierre would love to sign up. He's French but speaks perfect English. He's studying business management at the local college,' she said eagerly and Bernard chuckled and said: 'And is he as handsome as you are pretty?'

'Well, I think so, Mr Jensen,' she answered with a cheeky grin. 'And I don't think he'll be shy about taking his clothes off either.'

'Good, then I'd like to offer you and your boy friend places in the cast,' said Bernard crisply. 'We'll be shooting from nine o'clock tomorrow morning and we want to wrap it up in one day so you must be here by half-past eight sharp. I have hired a small coach to take us to the location which is only a few miles outside the town.

'Dress in casual clothes and, if you have a swimsuit, please bring it along. As it said in the advertisement, we'll pay you each fifty pounds for your services. You are free to work all day tomorrow, I take it? Good, then if you'll just read through this form and sign on the bottom line, it's a very straightforward contract. I'll give you a form for your friend and I'd like him to bring it back here by this evening if he wants to have a piece of the action.'

'Thank you very much,' said Belinda as she read through the contract which gave X-Ray Movies the sole rights to filmed material starring their artistes on payment of an agreed fee.

'Are there any questions you would like to ask me?' enquired the Dane and Belinda shook her head as she rose and followed him to the desk. Then as she was about to sign the contract, she wrinkled her brow as a thought suddenly struck her.

'Wait a moment, there is just one point I don't understand,' she frowned. 'Surely we'll never manage to learn our lines in time? Hadn't you better give me a script and I'll mug up as much as I can this evening.'

Bernard was clearly amused by the query, but he answered her question seriously, saying: 'That's won't be necessary, Belinda. We don't have a script as such. we simply tell the story to the cast and allow them to improvise their lines like they did in the days of silent films.'

Belinda still looked doubtful but he went on: 'Don't worry, we've never had problems with dialogue. Just say whatever comes into your head – if the worst comes to the worst, we can always edit it out.'

'Oh well, you should know,' she said as she signed the contract and folded a blank copy for Pierre and put it in the pocket of her skirt. 'Thanks again, Mr Jensen, I'd better be off.'

'Goodbye, Belinda, I'll meet you in the foyer tomorrow morning,' said Bernard as he escorted her to the door the telephone rang for the umpteenth time that morning.

After he had shut the door behind her he took the call which was from the hotel porter informing him that a Miss Summerfield was waiting for him in reception. 'Ask her to come up,' he instructed as he ticked off Belinda's name on his list. Maybe there was a special ingredient in the Sussex soil which accounted for there being so many attractive women in Falmington, said Bernard to himself. Besides Belinda and Pierre, he had already hired two other pretty girls and one guy, so now he really only needed perhaps one other girl and another man to complete the cast.

Yet three minutes later, as he shook hands with his

visitor, Bernard was thinking that perhaps he had been over-hasty in his judgement. Katie looked even more stunning than when he had met her in London at a party hosted by one of his British financial backers. She was dressed to kill with a skimpy white blouse which revealed the swell of her magnificent breasts and a pair of skin-tight jeans tucked into soft leather boots which accentuated her long legs and the tight rounded cheeks of her backside.

It took only minutes for them to agree an arrangement by which Katie would be allowed to take photographs during the filming at Sir Stafford Stiffkey's cottage the next day in exchange for a set of colour stills which Bernard could use as publicity shots for the movie which would be advertised in men's magazines throughout Europe.

'I wish that all my business negotiations were so easy,' Bernard remarked as he poured out two large vodkas and tonics from the small bar which he had instructed the staff to set up in his room. 'Usually when one is buying or selling, it is necessary to battle because any profit one earns will be at the expense of the other person, but here the deal is mutually beneficial.'

Katie accepted the drink and raised the glass to her lips. 'Cheers, Bernie. I think I understand what you're saying though Bruce, my boy friend, would be even more interested. He's a lecturer in modern business management at the London School of Economics.'

'So may I ask what brings you to Falmington?' asked Bernard. She shrugged her shoulders and answered: 'Bruce's work is so poorly paid that he's had to take a summer job at the local college here so that we can afford a decent holiday in September.'

Bernard allowed himself to smile when he thought of the collection of models, photographers, disc jockeys and minor pop stars who were among the guests at the party given by a producer. This was where he had been introduced to Katie the previous week. 'So he is an academic?' he continued. 'Please don't be offended if I say this surprises me. I would not have thought that a teacher would have fitted in with your friends I met at Fast Eddie Shackleton's party.'

It was Katie's turn to smile as she replied: 'You're absolutely right. The King's Road isn't Bruce's scene, but those kind of people aren't the crowd with whom I normally mix.'

And then she went on to explain that she was a State Enrolled nurse working for an eminent Harley Street specialist and had only been at Fast Eddie's party because she had been brought along by her cousin Joanna, who worked as a secretary for a leading artists and repertoire executive.

'Photography may only be a hobby,' Katie concluded. 'But if I say so myself, I have a good eye for a shot. frankly, with these new automatic cameras, a lot of the technical work is done for you.'

'Yes, I understand,' said Bernard as he tipped an ice cube and another double vodka into Katie's glass. 'However, I'm sure you would look terrific in front of the camera. Have you ever thought of taking up a career in modelling? You would earn much more money than in your present work.'

'Flattery will get you everywhere, kind sir,' she teased and then she let out a husky chuckle. 'Funnily enough, there was a photographer named Dave Pickering at Fast Eddie's who said the same thing to me and Joanna at a twenty first birthday party last year. What happened afterwards would have made a good scenario for one of your films.'

'Tell me more,' Bernard said encouragingly as he

moved across to sit next to her on the small settee. 'I'm always interested in any new storylines.'

Katie grinned: 'Well, if you use it you had better change the names to protect the guilty! Joanna and I were between boy friends at the time and so both of us were on the look-out for new men. After a while I spotted a nice-looking man of about thirty sitting on his own in a corner of the room. I pointed him out to Joanna and suggested that we go over and introduce ourselves to him. Well, we soon got chatting and he told us that his name was Dave and that he was a professional photographer.

'Joanna and I didn't let him continue for we had heard this line so often that we burst out laughing. Dave looked puzzled and Joanna explained; "Sorry, we didn't mean to be rude but if I had a pound for every time a fella's told me that he's a photographer and how I'd make a great glamour model, I'd be really rich!"

"Well, I *am* a photographer and actually both you girls would make super models," he said as he fished into his pocket and gave us both his business card. "Now are you satisfied?" he added but before we could answer, there was a great commotion on the other side of the room. Some stupid idiots had managed to gatecrash and when they had been told to leave, some fool swung a punch and then all hell broke loose.

"This looks like getting out of control, girls" said Dave as he put an arm round each of us and shepherded us out into the hall. "Come on, get your coats and I'll take you up to my studio for coffee. It's only round the corner and if things quieten down here, we can always come back later." Now neither Joanna nor me would normally go back to a guy's place only five minutes after meeting him, but he seemed like a nice boy and so we agreed to go with him. After all, we would be two against one and as

131

Joanna has a black belt in karate, we reckoned we would be safe enough!'

'And was Mr Pickering telling you the truth?' prompted Bernard and Katie nodded: 'Oh yes, Dave wasn't fibbing. He had a huge attic studio full of the latest equipment. He boiled up some water and made us coffee as promised and then afterwards Joanna asked him if he really thought that either of us could make a living as models. "Honestly, I think you would both make a fortune," he answered, scrambling to his feet. "And if you like, I'll prove it to you. All I need to do is to take a few test shots."

'He switched on the lights and laid down a fluffy green mat on a roll of white paper which covered the floor. "Come and sit on that together and we'll start from there," he said, looking very professional as he slipped in a roll of film into his Rolex.

'Joanna gave me a "I-will-if-you-will" look, but I had no objection to letting Dave take my photo, so we did as he asked and Dave started clicking away, getting us to pose this way and that. Often he would come over to us and adjust our clothing and I noticed that when he pulled our skirts up a little higher he let his hands linger on our thighs.

'Soon it was getting very hot under the powerful studio lights. Dave had already discarded his jacket and when he pulled off his shirt he revealed his broad bronzed chest. This made both Joanna and I rather horny. So much so that neither of us made any fuss when he tugged off our dresses over our heads. Dave unhooked Joanna's stretch Lycra bra and her full breasts came tumbling out as she sat on her haunches wearing only a tiny pair of frilly briefs over her tights. I hadn't put on a bra that night and hadn't bothered with tights either so all I had on was a pair of tiny white panties.

'Dave made me pose on all fours facing away from him then he got Joanna to sit astride my back but facing the camera. "Joanna, pull down Katie's knickers," he ordered and then with his eye on the viewfinder he added: "Now turn your face towards me, Katie so both your faces are showing. Super, that'll make a fantastic shot".

'It only took a minute or so for Joanna to lose her tights and panties and Dave posed us in progressively more suggestive positions, until we were finally in a nude *soixante neuf*. Then he slipped in a new film and added an extension lead and time switch to the camera before tugging down his trousers and pants and joining us on the rug.

'We rolled Dave over to his back and I sat astride his knees whilst Joanna sat perched on his chest. Next I moved down to lick the underside of his thick stiff cock whilst Joanna leaned forward and swirled her tongue all over his fat, uncapped helmet. Then Joanna thrust back her bottom until Dave Pickering was able to flutter his tongue around the wrinkled ring of her bum-hole and she yelped with pleasure when she felt the tip of his tongue tickle her in this secret little orifice.

'The three of us moved in unison and again and again Dave clicked the switch which activated the camera until he snorted with delight at his two-girls sucking-off and spurted his spunk into Joanna's mouth. She gulped down his jism and then I helped her lick his knob clean. When Dave had recovered he brought off Joanna with his tongue whilst he finger fucked my clitty until I came and we both slumped over his body.'

'I hope he gave you the negatives of all the photographs,' commented Bernard drily but Katie shook her head and laughed: 'No, because when we climbed off the mat and pulled out the time switch cord his jaw dropped and he clapped his hand to his head as he shouted: "Oh fuck it! The camera jammed and none of the threesome pix will have come out!" '

Bernard roared with laughter. 'I'll bet he was disappointed! It's just as well though, you wouldn't want any of those shots being shown around town.'

'No, I certainly wouldn't want that and the next day I resolved to stay behind the camera in future,' smiled Katie as she heaved herself up from the settee and shook hands with the Danish film-maker. 'So I'll meet you here at half past eight tomorrow morning. By the way, can I bring my boyfriend? He's dying to see how a movie is made.'

'Is this the economics teacher? Sure he can, so long as he keeps out of the way and doesn't interrupt the proceedings. Who knows, it's always useful to have another pair of hands available,' Bernard replied as he showed her to the door. 'Good to meet you, Katie, I'll see you tomorrow morning.'

After she left, Bernard studied the cast list again. Although he did not know it, along with Belinda Blisswood, he had hired Belinda's friend Sharon who worked for Bruce Teplin, Katie Summerfield's boy friend! The other girl to whom he had offered a job was a tall striking redhead named Josie Simpson so what with the two strippers from London, there would be no shortage of nude female flesh when the camera started rolling. Bernard picked up the telephone and asked the switchboard operator to hold all his calls.

As usual, it was more of a problem finding suitable men willing to show their wedding tackle on the silver screen. He was sure that Henry, the West Indian bouncer who would drive the strippers down to Falmington tomorrow morning, would have few inhibitions. But Bernard had no way of finding out whether Belinda's

French friend would perform satisfactorily. On the other hand he felt confident that Kent Bailey, the eighteen-year-old youth who he had signed up earlier this morning would turn up tomorrow morning. Oh well, he sighed, if the worst came to the worst, perhaps he could rope in Katie Summerfield's boy friend.

After dinner that evening, Denise Cochran marched into the foyer of the Berkeley Hotel and made her way to the reception desk where Belinda Blisswood was still on duty.

'No sign of Shane, I take it?' enquired Denise with an anxious edge to her voice. Belinda shook her head and replied: 'Not yet, but there's he's not expected in for at least another hour. Look, I have a fifteen-minute comfort break coming up at eight-thirty. Go and sit in the bar and have a drink and I'll join you there in a jiffy. I'll tell Carol to buzz us if "Mr Reynolds" checks in – oh, and if you're on expenses, I'll have a large gin and bitter lemon please!'

The bar was less than half full and Denise had no trouble finding an empty table. She ordered Belinda's drink and a scotch-on-the-rocks for herself. As she waited she surveyed the other customers at the bar and wondered whether the slim auburn-haired girl sitting alone in at a table near the window was Sandie Walters, the lass who had so captivated Shane Hammond.

Denise frowned as she considered whether or not to attempt to approach her. If she were Sandie, it might be useful to have already struck up a friendly conversation with her if she ever got as far as getting Shane to listen to her proposition. On the other hand, Sandie might just clam up and warn Shane that there was a woman downstairs asking questions about him. There would be little hope then of securing the rock star's attention, let alone his signature on a publishing contract.

According to Mike Glynn, the author of the topselling *I'll Make You A Million* self-help book which Denise had recently edited, it was a cardinal rule that taking positive action was always preferable than sitting back and doing nothing. Denise elected to take the plunge and find out whether this girl would respond to her overtures. However, just as she was about to rise from her seat, Belinda entered the bar and Denise decided to postpone the proposed *tête à tête* with Sandie till a little later in the evening.

'Wow, I see you took me at my word,' said Belinda as she settled herself into a chair and poured half the contents of the small bottle of bitter lemon into her gin. 'Cheers! I could really do with this – it's been a bloody long day and I'll be working tomorrow on my day off.'

'Oh you poor thing. Has Mr Swaffer asked you to put in some overtime?' Denise murmured sympathetically, which brought a crooked little smile to Belinda's face as she answered: 'Well, he did this afternoon, in a manner of speaking. I went to his office to look for some papers and found him in front of his desk, dressed only in tennis shorts, lifting up a pair of bar bells from the floor.

"So that's how you keep yourself trim, Andy," I said to him as I watched him raise them above his head. "Well, I'm sitting on my arse all day and don't get enough time for any real exercise," he grunted whilst he straightened his arms and held the bar bells above his head. "And I don't want to get as out of shape as some of our guests."

'He swung the bar bells down to the ground and when he leaned back against his desk, I had to admire his body which was muscular and well-developed with a hard, flat stomach. I think he must have noticed that I was getting turned on, because he said: "Of course, there are far easier ways of taking exercise. I've heard it said that a good fuck is the equivalent of a three-mile cross country run.''

'Honestly, Denise, I've no idea why all of a sudden I felt so horny – perhaps subconsciously I wanted to thank him for the marvellous climax I had when he fucked me the other afternoon when I wanted to find out details of Shane Hammond's booking. And I still don't really know what made me give him a sly wink and say: "Three miles, eh? And what's the equivalent distance of a blow job?"

"I can't say I know," he admitted and then with a wicked twinkle in his eye, he rubbed his palm between his legs and added softly: "But I'd very much like to find out."

'Well, that's all I needed to hear. I dropped to my knees in front of him and ripped off his shorts. Then taking his cock in my hand, I rubbed his hot, stiffening shaft against my cheek. It wasn't quite as thick as my boy friend Pierre's, but still a good size with a lovely red plum shaped helmet, perfect for sucking because I didn't have to stretch my lips too wide when I opened my mouth and started to gobble him.

'Anyhow, I took his prick between my lips. I loved the feel and taste of his hard tool as it slid to the back of my throat. For a moment or two I kept still and then I started to move my head slowly forwards and backwards as I grabbed hold of his bum cheeks whilst my head bobbed away.

'Every once in a while I took his cock out of my mouth and sucked his balls before popping his knob back between my lips when I felt them tightening up. That meant that he was ready to come and I moved my head faster up and down his shaft whilst I squeezed his balls. He shot off almost at once, grabbing the back of my head and holding it in place, though Andy needn't have worried – I wouldn't have pulled my mouth away from a spurting cock even if the bloody fire alarm had started to ring!

'His cock spasmed again and again, shooting spurt after spurt of creamy jism down my throat until it slowly softened and he leaned back against his desk, panting with exhaustion. I wiped the spunk from my lips with the back of my hand and looked up at him and said: "So what do you think, Andy? Is a blow job as good exercise as a good sprint?"

"I don't have enough data yet to make a fair comparison," he gasped, his chest still heaving with exhaustion. "I'm afraid we'll have to do this a few more times before I can give you a reasonable answer".'

Belinda gave a husky little laugh and gulped down her drink. 'Well, to cut a long story short, I went back to his office at four o'clock and I gave him another gobble. This time I'd slipped off my knickers so when I pushed him onto the floor and crouched over him, he was able to put his head under my skirt and lick me out whilst I sucked him off.'

Denise wrinkled her brow and said: 'And you've really no idea about what has given you such a craving to suck Andy Swaffer's cock?'

'Well, I suppose it could be something to do with the Danish guy here in the hotel who's come to Falmington to make a tit-and-bum movie,' said Belinda thoughtfully. 'Pierre and I have signed up to take part in it tomorrow. Fifty pounds each, cash in hand!'

'So that's what the advertisement in the local paper was about!' exclaimed Denise. 'Your friend Sharon's also gone for a part in that film. It'll probably be something on the lines of *Naked As Nature Intended*. If she gets a part you'll probably find yourself running around topless on the beach with her tomorrow morning.'

'I've got a fancy it might involve more than that for fifty

quid,' said Belinda darkly. 'Still, it'll be more fun jiggling my boobs at the camera if Sharon'll be there too. Good luck with Shane when he arrives, I'll be there to lend a hand if need be.'

A few minutes later Belinda left the bar. When Denise had formulated her plan of action she sauntered over with her drink in her hand to where the pretty dark-haired girl still sat alone with an empty glass on the table in front of her looking out anxiously towards the street.

'Hello there, it's Sandie Walters, isn't it?' she asked in a friendly tone of voice. Obviously startled, the girl looked up and stared at her whilst Denise continued: 'I hope I haven't disturbed you. I'm Denise Cochran and I'm in Falmington on one of the summer school courses at the College. Didn't we meet at the Shane Hammond concert?'

'I'm so sorry, I was miles away,' Sandie apologised as a slight flush appeared on her cheeks. 'Yes, I was at the concert but——'

'You don't remember seeing me,' finished Denise with a smile. 'Well, it's hardly surprising, the theatre was packed to the gills – and wasn't Shane terrific! But in fact, we were introduced at the reception here which Mr Swaffer gave for Shane and the band after the show.'

This was at best being economical with the truth. The fact of the matter was that although Denise had managed to wangle herself a ticket for the concert, she had not been invited to the strictly invitation-only party at the Berkeley.

'Yes, the concert was wonderful, though I can't remember too much about the party, Bernie and I were kept too busy to enjoy ourselves,' said Sandie, brushing back a strand of shining auburn hair which had fallen down the side of her face.

'Bernie?' queried Denise and Sandie continued:

'Bernie Gosling, my boss. He's the publicity manager of Falmington-On-Sea and we were looking after the press whilst Shane was in town. Bernie says he hadn't seen so many writers in town since the Horrobin sex scandal of 1962. Were you one of the journalists at the press conference?'

'No, I work in book publishing,' said Denise, deciding to throw caution to the winds as she accepted Sandie's invitation to sit next to her. 'In fact, that's the reason why I'm here this evening.'

And lowering her voice she added: 'Don't tell anyone, but Shane's coming back to Falmington tonight and while he's around I want a few words with him about his book.'

'He didn't say anything about a book to me,' said a puzzled Sandie and Denise affected surprise as she said: 'Oh, I didn't realise that you and Shane were close friends?'

'Not close friends, but we've kept in contact since the party,' Sandie replied with a worried look. 'I've written some letters to him and Shane's phoned me several times, but this will be the first time we'll have seen each other since we met at the party.'

She paused and tears formed in her eyes as she went on: 'It was all meant to be secret so we wouldn't be bothered by the press or any of the fans. If they find out that Shane's in Falmington we won't have any privacy at all and Shane might think it's all my fault that they found out. How did you know Shane was coming here? Only his manager knew about the arrangements and Lennie Lieberman wouldn't breathe a word to anybody.'

Denise neatly side-stepped the question as she assured the distraught girl that her secret tryst with Shane was safe. 'Don't worry, Sandie, I won't spill the beans. All I need is ten minutes with Shane tonight and I promise you that he's yours and yours alone for the rest of the weekend.'

'Oh, thank you, Denise, I'm so grateful,' said Sandie with great relief. 'I can't tell you how much I've been looking forward to this weekend. It would be awful if anything went wrong now.'

'No problem,' Denise rejoined as she patted her on the shoulder. 'And I suggest that when Shane arrives, you let me sort out my business with him. Then I'll be out of your way for the weekend.'

Shane Hammond would have preferred to drive himself down the A23 to the Sussex coast but, after he had miraculously escaped with only cuts and bruises after writing off his new Porsche on the MI earlier in the year, Lennie Lieberman had insisted that Shane sat in the back of the car on any journeys outside London. 'Barry will pick you up at half past seven on Friday evening in my car. You don't need wheels in Falmington so just tell him when you want him outside the hotel on Sunday afternoon to bring you home,' said his manager firmly in a voice that brooked no argument.

However, the rock star had not objected overmuch because he enjoyed the company of Lennie's nephew, Barry Abrahams who had horrified his parents by throwing up his job as a trainee solicitor to become chief roadie on Shane Hammond and the Hurricanes' whirlwind nationwide tours. Barry always had a good tale to tell and Shane was quite content to let him manoeuvre Lennie's Jaguar saloon through the crowded Friday-night London traffic.

And even more important was the fact that Barry could solve Shane's problem of how he could smuggle himself into the Berkeley. All he would have to do is wait in the car whilst Barry signed himself in as 'Mr Reynolds' and then come out and give him the key to his suite.

Barry Abrahams was only too happy to help out when Shane explained what he wanted him to do. 'Listen, you don't have to tell me how the girls drive you mad,' said Barry sympathetically as he joined the slow-moving queue of westbound traffic. 'Sure you have great fun and earn a fortune, but there's a downside too. Look, we're less than five minutes walk away from Craven Cottage – tell me, when was the last time you saw Fulham play? Even if you had the time, you couldn't stand with your mates behind the goal like I do at the Spurs.'

'That's a small price to pay, the way they're playing these days,' said Shane mildly. 'No, what really bugs me is not being able to live a normal life. Oh, I know I shouldn't grumble but you can appreciate that as I travel around the country all I get to see is the insides of hotel rooms and concert halls. The only people I ever get to meet outside the band and the roadies are record producers, reporters, dee-jays and the bloody groupies. Do you know, I haven't seen my Mum and Dad for almost three weeks?'

'Think yourself lucky, mate,' advised Barry with a husky grunt. 'If I don't call home at least twice a week, I think my Mum would go down to Golders Green nick and report me as a missing person! Still as I said to old Billy McFarlane, the chap who made all the arrangements for us when we were in Glasgow the other week, it really can't be much fun for Shane being cooped up in the hotel with at least half a dozen pretty birds queuing up to be pulled. Let's face it, he's going to disappoint at least four of his faithful fans.'

'Okay, wise guy, you can laugh but I can promise you that all six of those birds stayed outside and I just had a good night's kip all on my own,' Shane protested. He checked through his case to check that he had not forgotten to bring a copy of his proposed memoirs – for he had told Sandie that he wanted her to read and give her honest opinion on whether the script was worthy of publication.

Barry chuckled as he glided to a halt in the long line of cars waiting to cross Putney Bridge. 'I'll believe you. Billy and I were given great gobbles by two gorgeous sixteen-year-olds who had come all the way from Falkirk just to try and see you in the flesh. They couldn't get tickets for the show but they hung around the hotel in case you showed up, so Billy and I took pity on them so to speak.'

'Kindness is your middle name,' said Shane with evident sarcasm in his voice. 'Anyhow, I thought you had it away in Glasgow with that fair-haired girl who wrote for one of the Scottish newspapers?'

'You mean Laura, the chick from the *Evening Express*? Yeah, you're right, she was a great fuck though we didn't exactly hit it off straight away.'

'Dear, oh dear, was she disappointed at the size of your tiny cock?' teased Shane as he riffled through the sheets of his manuscript.

'Far from it. Any problems I've had with my John Thomas have come about because it's too large!' declared Barry as they inched forward a few yards towards the traffic lights. 'No honestly, Shane, it's the truth. When I used to play football at school, I was known as BB – Big Barry – and the lads used to whistle and cheer whenever they saw me in the shower. Of course, I didn't mind that at all, but some girls got a bit worried when they unzipped my trousers and took a look at my boner. That's what happened with Laura, by the way, after the press reception at the hotel. We had a few drinks and when I invited her upstairs to my bedroom she massaged my thigh as she said: "Sure, why not? I'm into Jewish guys as I prefer circumcised cocks".'

'Lucky old you,' murmured Shane but Barry was too involved in trying to squeeze through into a gap in the traffic to hear him and he continued: 'Well, as soon as we got to my room we started to smooch and by God did Laura have a lovely body. We made a game of taking off our clothes, nice and slow, though I could hardly wait to take off her top and get my hands on her creamy white breasts. She was only a petite little thing, not much over eight stone, but Laura was blessed with lovely large knockers and I sucked on her tawny tits whilst I helped her pull down her jeans. I was down to my underpants by the time I rolled down her knickers and rubbed my palm on her damp pussy. This set us both off, but when she ripped off my pants and saw my cock she gasped: "Christ Almighty, Barry, you're built like a gorilla! I've never seen such a big cock, you must have eleven inches of solid meat between your legs."

"Ten and a half, actually," I said modestly whilst she marvelled at my tower of power and said: "Bloody hell, even if it weren't so long, I don't think I'll ever get all that inside me. It's almost as thick as my arm."

'When I saw the hesitation in the expression on Laura's face I set about relaxing her by kissing her ear and massaging her breasts. This seemed to work for she soon began to moan and then she slipped her hand down to her pussy and started finger-fucking herself, saying: "My cunny will need to be sopping wet if you're ever going to be able to cram all of that massive cock inside me."

"Let me do the honours," I said and I buried my face in Laura's hairy cunt, sucking her clitty as if it were a strand of spaghetti. She started to thresh around as I brought her off and when I judged she was ready, holding my prick in my hand, I climbed over her and slid in my knob between her pouting pussy lips.

"Phew, I've never had anything like this inside my

crack, Barry," she panted whilst I felt her love channel open up for me. "Billy McFarlane has a huge cock but it's only a wee little stick compared to yours."

'I pulled out a little and then pushed back in again and when I only had to repeat this action a couple of times when Laura quickly caught my rhythm and jerked her hips upward every time I thrust forward. It took a few minutes for her love slit to get used to my massive member but like most pussies, Laura's cunt was marvellously elastic and I soon managed to stuff all my shaft into her juicy funnel. Then I increased the tempo and my balls slapped against her bum and we kept fucking like this until our bodies were soaked with sweat.

"A-h-r-e! A-h-r-e! That's incredible! I wish there was a mirror on the ceiling so I could see your cock pumping in and out of my pussy," Laura groaned as she wrapped her legs around my waist. I reached under her and rubbed my fingertip around the rim of her arsehole. This made her twist and buck like crazy as I rammed my cock harder and faster into her cunt whilst sliding my finger into her bum.

'Whilst my shaft was embedded in her cunt, I worked my finger and cock so that just as I withdrew my prick, I jabbed my finger up her bum up to the first knuckle.

"Yessss! Give it to me, Barry, cream my cunt with your jizz," she screamed out as she exploded into a mighty orgasm. I slammed my twitching tool into her sopping slit and shot a tremendous burst of spunk into her honeypot which sent Laura off again, but my poor prick was out for the count, which was hardly surprising – remember, I had already been gobbled by those two sixteen-year-olds from Falkirk.'

'Well, you certainly had a busier night in Glasgow than me,' sighed Shane and as they pulled away from a pedestrian crossing, Barry grunted: 'Maybe, but since then all I've used my cock for is to widdle with, and in my opinion——' He broke off to slam on his brakes to avoid a cyclist seemingly bent on committing suicide in Putney High Street and then rolling down the window, he screamed out: 'Watch out where you're going, you stupid fucker!'

As if by magic a policeman stepped out from between two parked lorries and gestured to Barry to pull over into the kerb. 'Oh no,' groaned the driver as the officer strode up purposefully towards him. 'That's all I need.'

'In a hurry, are we, sir?' queried the policeman, reaching inside his tunic pocket for his notebook. 'We don't appreciate people shouting out foul and abusive language in this part of the world.'

'Okay, okay, point taken, I apologise for shouting out,' said Barry testily. 'But that sodding cyclist swung out in front of me without looking and nearly caused an accident.'

Shane cleared his throat and came to Barry Abrahams' aid. 'He's not exaggerating, officer. Didn't you see what happened? No-one could have blamed my driver if the fellow had gone under our wheels.'

'That's not the point, sir, there was no need to use language,' began the policeman pompously and then as he peered inside he paused and said excitedly: 'Here, I know you. Aren't you what's-his-name, Shane Hammond?'

Shit, now poor old Barry is in for it, thought Shane. Only the previous week in Sheffield, a policeman had suffered a broken leg during a riot after one of the band's concerts and Shane had been heavily criticised by the local newspaper for not visiting the injured man in hospital. In fact Lennie Lieberman had written on his behalf to the unfortunate officer but in the rush to set up at their next venue, the letter had never been mailed.

So he gave a tired nod and raising his hand in surrender

he pleaded guilty to the charge. 'Yeah, but don't hold that against Barry. I swear to you that cyclist almost gave me a heart attack.'

'Oh, stuff the cyclist,' said the policeman, thrusting his notebook through the window. 'Could you give me your autograph, Shane? My girl friend Audrey is a great fan of yours. I took her to your gig at Wembley Town Hall last month for her eighteenth birthday.'

'Thank you, God,' murmured Barry as Shane answered: 'Of course I will – and she can have a copy of my new LP as a birthday present from me, I'll sign the sleeve for her. There you go, to Audrey with all my love, Shane Hammond, August 23rd, 1967. Tell her to keep this safe, in another eighteen years' time it'll be worth all of ten bob!'

He handed the record to the policeman and gave him back his notebook. 'Thanks, Shane, I'm really grateful,' said the officer as a long-haired girl in a well-fitted sweater and tight faded jeans stepped boldly out from the small crowd who had gathered on the pavement and cried out to a friend: 'Look, Eddie, I was right, it *is* Shane Hammond!'

'Oh no,' groaned Barry as the nubile girl wrenched open the door and asked Shane for an autograph. 'Sure,' said Shane, taking out a publicity photograph from his pocket. 'Who shall I sign it to?'

'Me,' replied the happy girl. 'My name's Tina. You couldn't sign one for my friend Beth could you?'

'Come on, Shane, we have to get going,' urged Barry as Shane searched in his pockets for another photograph. 'You wanted to be in Falmington by half past ten, remember?'

'Falmington?' squealed Tina. 'Why, that's where I'm going. Can you give me a lift, Shane? My boy friend was going to drive me down on his motor bike, but I'd do anything to travel down with you.'

At first the kind-hearted rock star shook his head, but then she begged him again to let her stay and he finally relented, saying: 'Well, so long as you promise to behave yourself.'

'Oh, I will, I will,' she said excitedly. 'Let me just tell Eddie that I won't need a lift after all.'

Fifteen seconds later she returned with a small ruck-sack tucked under her arm which Barry took from her and put next to him on the front seat. She slid into the back and sat proudly next to Shane as Barry slipped the clutch into first and saluted the grateful policeman, who held up his hand and stopped the traffic to let them ease into the stream of cars making their way out of London.

This was all too much for Tina who could hardly believe that she was sitting next to her idol. She blurted out: 'Oooh, am I glad I decided to see my old auntie this weekend. She'd asked me to come down and keep her company but I was thinking about putting my trip off till next Friday. Isn't it lucky that I didn't!'

Shane listened patiently to Tina's chatter till they drew clear of the London traffic and then Barry pulled over into a lay-by and brought the Jaguar to a stop. He turned round to Tina and said: 'Have you had any supper, love? I've a hamper in the boot with some sandwiches and a chilled bottle of wine. You're very welcome to join us – Shane's housekeeper always packs enough grub for an army.'

Barry was quite correct for as usual Mrs Moser had provided more roast beef sandwiches than even the three of them could eat. As Barry was driving, he contented himself with a Coke whilst Tina and Shane finished the excellent bottle of claret by themselves.

They climbed back in the car and Barry switched on the radio before gliding out back to the main road. 'We should be there inside an hour,' he commented. 'Why don't you two have a snooze whilst I listen to some music. On Radio 3, there's a record of Jascha Heifetz playing the Prokofieff G Minor Concerto that I really want to hear.'

'Blimey,' said a surprised Tina as she snuggled herself against Shane's shoulder. 'Are you into that highbrow stuff?'

'Barry's a talented violinist,' explained Shane, almost unconsciously sliding his arm round the soft curves of the frisky young girl. 'And I have to admit that he's taught me a lot about to listen to classical music. Believe me, once you're into Bach, Beethoven and Mozart, you get a great high listening to their work, like a good trip with a joint of Colombian Gold.'

'Well, I suppose there must be something in it,' Tina purred contentedly whilst she lifted her hand to undo the buttons on Shane's shirt. 'Eddie, my boy friend, is into classical music and he says it puts him in the mood for rumpy pumpy. Last Sunday we went out for a drive in the country in his Dad's car, and he was listening to something by some Czech with a funny name – what was it now––'

'Dvorak,' suggested Barry helpfully, and Tina giggled: 'That's the guy, you are clever. Anyhow, whilst Eddie was driving he made me sit close to him and play with his cock. Whilst I was jacking him off, he began to talk about all the different ways we were going to make love once he found a place to park the car. He was deliberately driving me crazy because he knew that talking like that would also make me horny. Sure enough my pussy soon started to get damp and I began to undress him even though we had stopped at some traffic lights. God knows what the people in the car on our left thought if they saw me pull down his trousers and pants, but Eddie just chuckled as he pulled away quickly from the lights. A couple of minutes later he was driving through Wimbledon Common with nothing on from the waist down.

'He pulled into a quiet lay by and in a flash I was bending over him and sucking his slippery wet cock. By now I was so hungry for his dick that I could have eaten it! I deep throated him whilst he finger-fucked my bum with his free hand and somehow we managed to come together. Next we climbed into the back seat I undressed and Eddie licked me out whilst his prick recovered from my blow job. Thank goodness, it only took a few minutes before his cock stiffened up again and then, kneeling on the car seat, he lifted my ankles onto his shoulders and teased me by fisting his own hand up and down his shaft, making me beg him to slip it into my cunt.'

'I hope he obliged in the end,' murmured Shane and she nodded: 'Oh sure, he just wanted to hear me beg for it. I threw back my head and groaned: "Fuck me, Eddie, fuck me with your thick prick, you randy stud!" and he mounted me and slid his shaft between my love lips deep inside my sticky honeypot. Eddie's a passionate lover and he made the car judder and he started to pump in and out of my sopping juice box. I was so aroused that I came almost straight away and yelled out: "Shoot your load, Ed, empty your balls. Drench my cunt with your creamy spunk!"

'He cupped my bum cheeks in his hands and then his throbbing tool jetted a gush of semen into my cunt which splashed against the folds of my pussy and dribbled down my thighs to mingle with my own love juices on the back seat of his Dad's car. We lay kissing and cuddling and Eddie pulled out his soft cock whilst I wiped my pussy with my panties. Then I slipped my finger into my pussy and asked Eddie to lick off our juices whilst I washed his knob with my tongue.'

Tina paused and then added with a dramatic flourish:

'And seconds later I had the most frightening experience of my life.'

Despite his devotion to the strong, lyrical music of Prokofieff, Barry had been listening attentively to Tina's tale. He turned his head and enquired: 'Don't tell me, Eddie had left off the handbrake and the car started rolling backwards.'

'No, it was something much worse than that,' she replied. 'There was a loud tap on the window and there was a uniformed policeman peering in at us. Eddie just had time to fling my dress over me when the copper opened the door and said to us: "Get dressed, you two and then come out of the car. I'm arresting you both for gross indecency in a public place."

"Oh no, this'll be in all the papers," I moaned as white-faced, Eddie heaved himself on top of me. Then a wild idea went through my mind. "Stay where you are, Eddie" I said as I opened the door and stood stark naked in front of the policeman, running my hand through my damp muff of pussy hair.

"Surely we could come to some arrangement, officer?" I cooed invitingly as I started to stroke myself. It wasn't difficult to make myself wet again for he was only a young bobby and I thought that he must have been almost as embarrassed as Eddie when I reached out and rubbed my palm against his cock, because there was little stirring there.

"Wouldn't you like to fuck me instead?" I asked as I continued to frig myself. "No? Well, perhaps you would prefer to watch my boy friend fuck me instead? Come over here, Eddie."

'Well, Eddie wasn't too keen at first but he realised that this was our best chance of getting out of trouble so, still bollock naked, he slowly walked towards me. The policeman said nothing as I grabbed hold of Eddie's shaft and rubbed it up and down until it began to thicken and his beautiful round helmet was uncovered as his foreskin snapped back and his cock became as hard as a rock. Then I heard the young policeman panting, but not guessing for a second what had turned him on, I called out: "Come on, copper, come and join us."

'With a hoarse cry he ran over to us, dropped to his knees and pulled my hand away from Eddie's cock. Without so much as a by your leave, he started to suck his throbbing tool which was bobbing about in front of his face. He lathered his tongue around my boy friend's swollen shaft, moving his head forwards and backwards as poor Eddie shot me a helpless look. "Close your eyes and pretend it's me," I hissed at him, "Anything's better than being arrested."

'To make it easier for Eddie I crawled on all fours between his bum cheeks and after giving them a good licking, I squeezed his hairy balls. This did the trick and Eddie came into his mouth, sending a stream of spunk down the young copper's throat which he gulped down with relish.

'Then all he said was: "My sergeant is supposed to meet me here in five minutes and so you'd better be away smartish – and don't come back later as we're on patrol all day." So what do you think of that?'

Barry chuckled: 'Well, as Brendan Behan said about the British police, they're the best that money can buy! Seriously though, Tina, there must be queers in every walk of life, so we shouldn't be that surprised. So long as he kept his side of the bargain, does it really matter that he fancied your boy friend more than you?'

'No, I don't suppose it does, though it doesn't do much for a girl's pride when a guy fancies her boy friend more than her!' she said as she tried to unzip the zip on Shane's trousers. Although he had been aroused by her story, the rock star was now thinking more about the delights which would soon be offered by Sandie Walters in Falmington-On-Sea and gently pushed her hand away. 'Sorry love, but I never fuck on a first date,' he said. In the driving mirror, though, Barry had caught the expression of disappointment in Tina's eyes. He signalled a right turn and pulled the Jaguar into a used car lot.

'Here, what the blazes are you doing?' asked Shane crossly as Barry switched off the engine and opened his door. The driver ran round to the opposite side of the car and opened the back door to slide next to Tina. 'Look here, Shane, this lovely girl needs shagging and if you're not prepared to do the job, I am.'

Shane expelled a deep breath as Tina unbuckled her belt and lifted her bum to allow Barry to slip down her jeans. Truth to tell, she would have far rather had Shane Hammond's sophisticated shaft between her thighs than Barry Abrahams' colossal circumcised cock, but recounting her story had made her hot to trot, and Tina wondered whether Shane could be persuaded to join in the fun later.

So she pulled her sweater over her head and asked Shane if he would kindly unhook her bra. He performed this task and freed her firm young breasts and perky red nipples which stood out almost impudently like two succulent raspberries. But then, to Tina's chagrin, he opened the door of the car. 'Make it quick, I'm going to take a walk, I'll be back in five minutes,' he snapped.

Sod it, perhaps he'll watch through the windows, she muttered to herself as Barry rolled down her panties and exposed her fleecy bush of pussy hair. He pulled Tina to him and smashed her jouncy boobs against his chest. He kissed her passionately and a shiver ran up her spine when his hand snaked between her legs and caressed her moist mount.

'Oooh, you're very wet,' breathed Barry as she sensuously moved herself across the seat and murmured: 'Lick me out, lover and then you can fuck me. How does that sound?'

'Perfect, absolutely perfect,' he grunted and Barry heaved himself up to straddle her, his knees resting on the soft leather of the seat as, without further preliminaries, he dived down. He dipped his tongue between her yielding outer lips into the crevice of her folds which were usually petite and pink but which were now swollen with pleasure. He ran his tongue up and down the slippery grooves of her crack and she was so juicy that her love juices welled in the opening of her love channel so strongly that even when he licked them away they filled up again immediately.

'Aaargh! You've got it!' Tina cried out in delight as he found the tiny button under the fold at the base of her clitty. He began to twirl his tongue around it and, pushing his mouth up against her clinging cunt, Barry moved his head back and forth along the length of her soaking slit and lapped up the cuntal juice which was now running freely down her thighs. With each stroke of his tongue, she arched her body in ecstasy, pressing her erect clitty up to meet his fluttering tongue. The pungent aroma of her pussy now filled the Jaguar as, with a heartfelt throaty sigh, she achieved her climax.

Barry lifted his head and scrambled to his knees as he unzipped his flies and pulled out his colossal stiff cock. 'Stone me, what a size! I don't think I could take such a monster in my tight little puss,' she gasped as she jerked both hands up and down his veiny shaft, faster and faster until he gave a piteous moan and a fountain of sticky jism burst out of his cock. She continued to manipulate his pulsating prick until she had milked him dry.

He gave Tina a box of paper tissues which were kept on

the back shelf and then rummaged in his pocket for a handkerchief on which he wiped his cock. There was a sudden sharp knock on the window and for a moment Tina thought history was about to repeat itself, but to their relief it was only Shane who opened the door and said sharply: 'Come on, you two, I promised to meet someone in Falmington at half past ten and I don't want to be late.'

'Don't worry, you'll be there well before then,' grunted Barry whilst he climbed back into the front seat. Shane opened the door and wrinkled his nose as he slid in.

'Well, you can explain the smell and the stains on the back seat to your Uncle Lennie,' he said in a rather unfeeling tone to Barry who muttered an inaudible few words in reply as he switched on the engine and pulled out sharply from behind the line of used cars to rejoin the main road.

When they reached Falmington, Barry dropped Tina off opposite the pier and then gunned down the sea-front to the Berkeley. 'Sorry about the delay, Shane, but I really enjoyed myself in the used car lot – and see, it's still only five past ten. Believe me, she'll be waiting for you.'

'Who says there's a girl waiting?' demanded Shane irritably, but when through the large wide window he saw Sandie sitting in the bar, his mood brightened. He went on: 'Sorry, Barry, I didn't mean to snap. I'm just a bit frazzled these days. Be a pal and just sign in for me, then you can bring the key back to me and scoot off back to London.'

'No problem, I won't be a minute. What's the alias you're using?'

'Michael Reynolds, you know, the guy who made a fortune from those miniature Japanese TV sets.'

Shane only had to wait a short time before Barry returned and gave him the key to his suite. 'Here you are, sir, room number three hundred and sixty nine – a very appropriate number in the circumstances.'

'We live in hope,' said Shane with a grin. 'Thanks for the lift, chum. Lennie said you'll be back here on Sunday at half past seven.'

'Half seven on the dot,' Barry promised as he handed his passenger his black overnight bag. 'Er, Shane, do me a favour, if Uncle Lennie happens to call you early tomorrow morning and asks where the hell I've got to, would you tell him that as I was feeling tired, I decided to stay the night in Falmington and I'll be with him by midday at the latest.'

Shane smiled as he answered: 'Of course I will, mate. You wouldn't be planning to shoot over to Tina's auntie for a night-cap, I suppose?'

'That had crossed my mind,' admitted Barry with a wink. 'Cheers, Shane, see you on Sunday.'

'Bye, Barry,' said Shane. He ducked his head down and hurried through the swing doors and reception lobby, aiming to get to his room as quickly as possible so that he could call reception and ask someone to tell the pretty auburn haired girl in the bar that Mr Reynolds had arrived and was waiting to see her.

However, as he entered the lift, seemingly out of the blue, two attractive girls followed him inside. One, a stunning blonde was dressed in the hotel uniform of a black jacket and short skirt. She was holding a file in her hand as she pressed the third floor button. 'Thank you very much,' he said, and then the other girl, a long-legged beauty dressed in a tight green mini dress said: 'Our pleasure, Mr Hammond, but in return we would appreciate a very quick word with out.'

How the hell did they recognise me, wondered Shane,

as he growled: 'Leave it out, please, I'm here on private business.'

'Yes, and as I said only half an hour ago to Sandie Walters, your visit to Falmington will stay completely private if you'll just give us ten minutes of your time,' said the attractive girl in the green dress. 'Then you won't hear or see from us again throughout the whole week-end.'

In other words, you'll tell the bloody press where I am, said Shane to himself. If she wasn't so bloody pretty I'd tell her to fuck off. But that wouldn't really help, he reasoned, as she obviously knew about his friendship with Sandie. Damn it, they have me over a barrel, he thought, and he would do best to go with the flow. So he gave a brief sigh and, giving in graciously, he said: 'All right, girls, you win, but ten minutes max, okay?'

'I don't think we'll need to keep you any longer than that,' said the girl in the green dress. 'So let's get down to business. My name is Denise Cochran and this is Belinda Blisswood.'

'Pleased to meet you both,' muttered Shane as they reached the door of his suite. He unlocked the door and stood aside politely to let the girls march through in front of him.

'I hope you like the suite because I chose it for you myself,' said Belinda proudly. 'This is the best accommodation in the hotel. I know you're used to staying in five-star de luxe places but at least you have a sea-view and the bed's very comfortable.'

Shane gave her a friendly grin and said: 'And do I also thank you for the bowl of fruit and the bottle of champagne in the ice bucket?'

'No, they're from Mr Swaffer,' she admitted as Shane sat on the bed and said: 'Well, it's still very nice, Belinda, thank you for your trouble. Now what can I do for you?'

She smiled back and pulling his latest LP from the folder under her arm, she said: 'Oh, all I want is an autograph, please. I love your music, Shane, and I hope it's not true you're going to split with the Hurricanes.' He laughed as he took the record from her. 'You must have read that piece about Matt Mostra in the *Daily Sketch*,' he commented as he signed the LP with a flourish. 'All Matt said was that he was going to record a few instrumentals with the group. We've no intention of splitting up – at least, none that I know about!'

He unzipped a small pocket inside his bag and brought out two tickets which he gave to Belinda with her LP and added: 'Here, I'm also giving you two complimentary tickets to our concert at the Odeon, Hammersmith in October. If you can make use of them, come round backstage after the show for a drink and you can meet the boys in the band.'

'Oh Shane, you are kind. That would be wonderful,' said Belinda happily. He gave her a friendly kiss on her cheek whilst he steered her to the door. 'I can easily get any day off I want after the summer season rush. Now I'll be off and you won't see me again till October – and don't worry, once you're through with Denise, I'll make sure that you and Sandie won't be bothered by anyone again.'

She returned his kiss whilst he opened the door and Shane waved goodbye before closing it. Then he turned round to Denise and said grimly: 'Right, now what can I do for you? Something tells me that you're not going to be as easily pleased as Belinda.'

Denise grinned and without wasting any further time told him of her company's interest in his memoirs. Shane listened gravely and then scratched his head. 'Well, I'm flattered that Chelmsford and Parrish want to publish my book. Wasn't that the firm which brought out that saucy novel by Erica Bolyn recently? I enjoyed reading it and then I gave it to my Mum and she loved every word.'

'You read *A Delightful Scandal*?' said Denise with some price. 'I'm really pleased you liked it.' She went on to explain how she had rescued the unsolicited manuscript from oblivion and edited the raunchy novel which had shot into the bestseller lists a week after publication and was already reprinting for the third time in a month.* 'C and P is only a small house but everyone there would put our hearts and souls into making your book the biggest publishing event of the year.'

He smiled at the earnest, pleading expression on her face. Although he would have liked to have made her ecstatic by agreeing to let Chelmsford and Parrish publish his book, he was sensible enough to realise that he could not make such a commitment at this stage. 'The book's not even finished and it's a bit of a mish-mash at the moment,' he said, walking over to the dressing table and picking up the folder of writing paper and envelopes which the Berkeley provided for their guests in every room. 'But I'll tell you what I'll do for you, Denise Cochran. The book's not finished yet, but I'll jot down a note this very minute to my literary agent Beth Macdougall to tell her that I want Chelmsford and Parrish to have first refusal on the book – but on the condition that you work on any editing that needs to be done.

'By the way, your bosses will be pleased to know that I'm not looking for a huge advance,' Shane remarked as he began writing the letter to his agent. 'Beth and Lennie Lieberman are so confident that it will be a bestseller that they've told me I'm far better off tax-wise to spread the royalties over a period of time. Mind you, what Beth thinks isn't an over-the-top advance might not be the

---

* See 'Summer School I: Warm Days, Hot Nights' [New English Library]

same kind of figure which your people have in mind!'

Denise had been stunned into silence by the ease of accomplishment of her mission but now she gave a little nervous laugh and said: 'Beth Macdougall is one of the best agents in London and I'm sure she'll get the best kind of deal for you.'

'Well, I'm not going to be involved in the negotiations,' said Shane as he folded the sheet of notepaper and slid it into an envelope. 'I'm not even going to post this letter but I'm giving it to you to send to Beth. I've written that a girl named Denise will contact her very shortly and I leave it to you and Beth to work something out between you.'

'It's very kind of you, Shane, I only hope you won't be too disappointed if——,' she faltered as she put the envelope in her bag, but placing his forefinger on her lips, he interrupted her and said softly: 'It may sound foolish – and it probably is a very stupid way to do business – but don't you ever have strong feelings about people only minutes after you've met them? I don't exactly mean love at first sight, but I usually know after less than thirty seconds whether a particular person is going to click with me, and I just know somehow that you and I are going to get on together.'

There was a moment's pause. They both felt themselves being carried forward by a strange irresistible force as Denise raised her face to the handsome rock star and within seconds of the first taste of her warm lips, Shane's tongue had gained entrance and was exploring the delicious welcoming cavern of her mouth in a long seeking kiss.

For an instant they clung together and then Denise broke away and murmured: 'Shane, I think you've forgotten that Sandie is patiently waiting for you downstairs.'

He nodded and immediately apologised. 'I'm sorry, Denise, it just seemed so natural to kiss you. I told you that first impressions count for everything as far as I'm concerned. As soon as you began talking about my book, I had this gut feeling that we'd make a great team.'

'Well, I'd love to find out if you're right – workwise, that is,' she hastily added as she fought against the impulse to hug him again. She picked up her handbag and, after blowing him a kiss, sidled quietly out of the door. Shane picked up the telephone to call Belinda and inform her that Sandie Walters could come up to his suite as soon as she liked. He felt slightly ashamed that the thought had ever crossed his mind – as lovely as Sandie Walters was, what a wonderful time he would have in Falmington if he could persuade the sexy Denise to join them for a three-in-a-bed romp.

Nevertheless, an hour or so later, all such troilistic thoughts had been banished from his brain as he lay in bed with Sandie, their warm naked bodies slithering wetly together as he sucked her tongue into his mouth.

Despite her demure appearance, to his surprise, Sandie turned out to be a veritable tigress between the sheets. She growled with passion as Shane cupped her breasts in his hands, feeling their jouncy firmness as he ran his palms over her horned up tawny nipples. He licked each raised tittie with the tip of his tongue till they stood out like two little red bullets whilst she reached down to his throbbing tool and gave his shaft a loving squeeze.

'Now I want you inside me – all the way,' she whispered fiercely. Still holding his rigid penis in one hand, she turned herself over onto her tummy and with her free hand, slid a pillow down the bed to rest under her hips. Then she released his cock as Shane scrambled to his knees behind her. He drew a deep breath as he parted her deliciously tight rounded buttocks and placed his knob inside the smooth crevice between her impudent young bum cheeks. His lascivious gaze travelled down from the wrinkled rosette of her arsehole to the pouting lips of her cunny crack, unsure into which orifice to place his pulsating prick.

However, Sandie solved this problem for him by turning her head and murmuring: 'Don't go up my bum, Shane, it's my pussy which needs a good seeing to.' This slightly disappointed him as he was rather taken with the idea of jamming his knob inside the brown puckered opening. For some odd reason an old school playground rhyme came into his head: *One up the bum will make them cum, one up the rectum won't affect them*.

But he didn't argue and, holding his tadger in his hand, Shane guided his cock home in one delicious thrust, embedding his knob inside Sandie's clinging wet cunt until his pubic curls were pressed against the soft globes of her beautiful bottom.

She was warm, wet and very willing and she breathed fiercely as he began to fuck her in a slow, forceful rhythm. Then Sandie caught his pace and answered his pelvic jabs in time with his pounding pole. He slewed his stiff truncheon forwards and backwards with his hands clasped round her body to cup her jiggling breasts.

'Fuck me, Shane, fuck me,' she moaned. He managed to slam his shaft in and out of her squelchy love hole for a further two minutes and then he tensed up with the approach of his oncoming orgasm. She felt his cock quiver inside her love channel and then, grinding her backside against his thighs, she panted: 'Now, Shane, now, fuck me hard and fast. I want to feel all of you, right up to your balls!'

'You got it, baby,' he grunted as he creamed her cunny with jet after jet of warm sticky jism. Sandie yelled with excitement and wiggled her bum from side to side, shuddering with pleasure as the force of her own climax swept through her body.

Shane slumped back on the bed but Sandie's blood was up and she was eager to continue their lustful joust. She smoothed her hand over his flat belly and into the curly growth of dark pubic hair. She looked reverently down to his flaccid penis which now hung limply over his thigh and pulled down his foreskin to expose his rounded pink knob. She kissed his cock and then pumped her head up and down the shaft as she fondled his balls. But his tool only twitched until she stuck her finger up his bum and in seconds his cock jumped up to attention.

Sandie smiled at the result of her handiwork and slipped her hand up and down the glistening shaft, delicately frigging his cock as she hauled herself up on her knees and leaned forward to plant a luscious moist kiss on his uncapped helmet. A sigh of ecstasy escaped from Shane's throat as she sucked three full inches of his cock into her soft mouth, her lips straining to encircle the thick shaft.

He thrilled to the most delicious sensations as she slid her mouth juicily up and down his palpitating cock, her gleaming auburn curls bouncing as she kept her lips taut on his veiny length, kissing, licking and lapping until she knew he was ready to explode. For an instant she withdrew her lips in case he wanted to plunge his prick back into her tingling cunt.

But Shane's penis stood like an appetising fleshy lollipop. A tremor of raw desire crackled through Sandie's body and she swiftly popped his knob back between her lips. She gently pressed his balls and began to swallow in anticipation of the sticky gush of spunk which she knew would soon be coursing out of his cock at almost thirty miles an hour, according to the sex quiz in one of the daring new women's magazine which had just come onto the market.

She curled her tongue around the crown of his cock and made no attempt to withdraw when Shane groaned and the first jet of frothy seed spurted out into her mouth. Sandie gulped down his tangy emission with genuine relish, milking his balls of every last drain of spunky love juice.

They locked together for a silent minute and then Sandie started to rub herself sensuously against him.

'How about a little more nookie?' she cooed as she squeezed his shrunken shaft. Shane's jaw dropped: 'Christ, love, I'm not up to it. The Hurricanes' drummer, young Matt Mostra, says he can do it three times without stopping if he's really in the mood, but just two goes on the trot knackers me out these days.'

Now Sandie's face fell and she swiftly let go of his limp member. 'Oh, I'm sorry! I'm always feeling horny just after my period,' she apologised but Shane shook his head and went on: 'No, there's nothing to be sorry for. Letting your fella know you want him is the best compliment you can pay any guy. It's a myth though that all guys are always ready for a spot of rumpy. It just isn't true, believe me.'

'So that story about your making love to six girls in one night which I read last month in the *Daily Sketch* wasn't true?' enquired Sandie as a roguish smile played about her lips.

'Of course it wasn't true. What do you think I am, Superman? Our publicity people placed that story in the papers because Lennie Lieberman thought I needed a more outrageous profile to keep the kids' interest.'

Sandie nodded slowly as she digested this information and then, with a twinkle in her eye, she said: 'Well, they say you should never believe what you read in the papers.

You'll be telling me next that your romance last year with that dee-jay Karen Thomson was also a made-up tale.'

'This may be a terrible cliché but Karen and I are just good friends,' laughed Shane as he playfully smacked her bottom. 'Now that's more than enough about me. Let's open the bottle of champagne in that ice-bucket and you must tell me all your news.'

At the same time on his bedroom two floors up from Shane Hammond's suite, Bernard Jensen was also popping open a bottle of champagne. Without spilling a drop, he poured the bubbly golden wine into the glass held out by Josie Simpson, the strikingly tall girl who was sitting on his bed dressed in a white halter-neck dress which appeared to be moulded to her lithe slender body. She was not wearing a bra and Bernard shot an admiring glance at the dark protruding points of her nipples beneath the thin fabric.

This was the girl he had finally chosen to star with Belinda Blisswood, Sharon Shaw and the two strippers from London on the set tomorrow. She was a bright girl who had obtained a first-class degree in sociology from the University of Sussex and was now busy writing her thesis on *The Changing Sexual Mores in England During The Early Years Of The Twentieth Century* for her doctorate. Josie lived with her boy-friend, a senior barman at one of the town's busiest pubs, and to supplement her income, she worked sixteen hours a week as an artists' model for the advanced painting class at Falmington College of Higher Education.

Josie was a shrewd enough girl to realise how best to charm Bernard Jensen when she went to the Berkeley to meet him. She had adjusted her tight-fitting dress to expose the maximum amount of cleavage and adopted a softer, breathier tone of voice for her interview. She did not mention the fact that she was a postgraduate student, for Josie cynically maintained that the last thing most men needed was for some smart girl to make them feel even more insecure than they already were. With a man, she maintained, flattery will get you everywhere – from his performance in bed to his ability behind the wheel of a car.

As it happened, Josie herself had been genuinely charmed by the suave Dane. It was her suggestion that she returned to the hotel later that evening so that they could chat about the film, although she had no illusions of its probable content.

'Look, I suppose that I'm an exhibitionist at heart and have no objections to showing off my body,' she told Bernard as she fluttered her long eyelashes. 'To be honest, it gives me quite a thrill to think of all those men getting hard-ons whilst they're looking at my tits – but having sex on screen is another matter.'

'We could never put out a movie of that kind in Britain. Most police forces turn a blind eye to what's being screened at film clubs but anything really raunchy would be stamped on pretty quickly,' remarked Bernard, trying to address Josie's qualms. But he had no intention of telling her of the no-holds-barred version he hoped to make for the lucrative Middle East market where the oil rich sheiks would pay handsomely for blue films.

'In any case, we have two strip-tease girls arriving from London tomorrow and they'll take care of any scenes which you might consider rather too rude for you to take part. As I said to you this morning, so long as you're broad minded, I don't see any problems.'

Josie giggled sweetly as she picked up her handbag and said: 'Oh, I'm broad-minded all right and I'm really looking forward to tomorrow. My star sign is Taurus and

in the paper this morning Gypsy Lionel said that Taure-
ans are restless for adventure. We should use our imagi-
nation to liven up our social lives. I tried doing that last
week when my boy-friend bought a new camera and I
posed for him early one morning down on one of the
quiet little beaches along the Brighton Road. Would you
like to have a look at them?'

'Sure,' he replied, and Josie passed a folder of colour
prints over to him. Bernard looked with interest at the
first picture on top of the pile. It showed Josie standing
smiling seductively at the camera dressed in a faded
denim jacket, tight blue jeans and a pair of calf-high
white boots. The second shot showed her with the denim
jacket off and leaning forward slightly with the top
buttons of her white shirt undone so that Bernard was
given an excellent view of the creamy swell of her breasts.
The next picture showed her sitting in the sand pulling off
her boots. As he expected, Josie discarded her shirt for
the following shot in which she was shown proudly
displaying her small but perfectly formed uptilted breasts.

'Did you say your boy friend took these photographs?'
enquired Bernard as he pored over a picture of Josie
wriggling out of her jeans.

'Yes, Phil's quite a talented lad, don't you think?' she
replied, moving closer to Bernard to look at the photographs over his shoulder. 'He's never studied photography but he has a good eye for a shot which is something
that can't really be taught.'

'Absolutely so, you can only explain the rules but
technique is something innate,' agreed Bernard as he
continued to pore over the remainder of the photographs
which showed Josie's beautiful body in sharp, crisp focus.

He studied the last print in the pack with special care as
he murmured softly: 'This is very good indeed.' He stared
at the sensual shot of Josie who had her back to the

camera with her head turned round to the side and a bright smile on her face. She was naked except for a minute pair of string bikini panties, the narrow strap of which disappeared into the crevice between her dimpled bare buttocks. Bernard's cock was by now standing as stiff as a poker and his hand trembled slightly when he returned the photographs to his guest.

'So you see, I'm no prude,' said Josie as she slipped the photographs back into her bag, 'although you may think me very unadventurous. Whilst some people like fucking in trains, offices, and even shops – I've a friend who likes to screw in the fitting rooms when she goes out with her boy friend to buy some clothes. Now I adore a good fuck but what I find the most satisfying way of making love is in bed and with my man in what we call the missionary position.'

She gave a little giggle and went on: 'I don't know how you say that in Danish,' but Bernard swallowed hard and said huskily: 'It's all right, I know exactly what you mean.'

'I'm sure you like shagging too, Bernard,' she declared and, not waiting for a reply, she pulled her dress up to her chin, exposing two stunningly proportioned breasts which quivered enticingly in front of him like ripe fruits. 'Any-how, I always thought that fucking was the Danish national sport.'

Bernard let out a husky chuckle as he gulped down the rest of his drink and said: 'What makes you say that, Josie? Have you ever been to Denmark?'

'Oh yes, I went for a cycling holiday there with Phil last summer and I had a fine time too. Unfortunately that was more than could be said for Phil because before we had left Copenhagen he rode the wrong way down a one way street and was knocked off his bike! He was lucky not to have been killed, but one of his ankles was badly wrenched and he hit his head on the pavement and so finished up in hospital with concussion. I wanted to stay with him but he insisted I took off for a couple of days and so armed with a map I made my way out into the lovely Danish countryside.

'Of course I was sorry for Phil lying there all alone in hospital, but the thought of having myself and no-one else to think about was refreshing and the sensation of the hard saddle between my legs pressing into my pussy was even better!

'Anyway, that night I rode into a camp site and a friendly young couple helped me pitch my tent next to theirs. Like almost all the Danish people I met, they spoke perfect English and when they found out that I was all on my own, they invited me into their tent for supper. I had brought with me a half bottle of Johnnie Walker from the duty-free shop on the boat and after a few drinks we became very gossipy. The pretty girl, whose name was Brigitte, told me that she and George were both seventeen and still in their final year at school. They lived in Copenhagen with their parents who were very strict and so the only way they could sleep together was to go cycling every weekend in the summer!

'The whisky was now having an effect on all of us and they cuddled up together and George slid his arm around Brigitte and squeezed her left breast. Looking at the couple I felt very envious because George might have only been seventeen, but he was of a hunky build, and when Brigitte lovingly stroked the bulge in the front of his shorts, I found myself wondering about whether his penis was as well developed as his muscles. I became even more aroused when Brigitte slipped her hand down and began to rub his cock. I could hardly wait to thank them for their hospitality and then rush back to my tent to jerk myself off.

'Well, I stripped off and was about to start caressing my tingling pussy when I heard some familiar sounds coming from George and Brigitte's tent. The thought of this young couple screwing away only a few yards away made me so horny that I just had to see for myself exactly what they were up to.

'I slipped on a tee-shirt and crept outside to peer through the flap of their tent. As I had guessed, Brigitte was being well and truly fucked. She was lying on a mattress with her legs wrapped round George's back as he lay still, his cock sheathed inside her quim. But before long he started to jerk his hips to and fro and I watched his thrilling young cock slide in and out of Brigitte's juicy cunt.

'Suddenly she opened her eyes and looked at me straight in the eye. I stepped back in horror. However, I need not have worried for Brigitte was far from being annoyed – indeed she appeared to be quite pleased that I had been watching them. Neither did George seem to be embarrassed, for he simply turned round and invited me to join if I so wanted.

'Then as if to encourage me, he pulled his prick out of her pussy and swapped places with Brigitte who sat on his face. Leaning forward to take his thick tadger into her mouth, she then signalled to me to get down and start licking with her. At first I hesitated and then I thought to myself, what the heck? George was soon moaning with delight as two wet tongues slid up and down his throbbing shaft.

'My cunt was now on fire and I slipped my hand between my legs and plunged my fingers inside my own sopping snatch. "You can have George's cock fuck you if you prefer," said Brigitte generously as she sat up so that George could lick out her creamy cunt. I straddled the boy and eased myself down on his rock-hard rod and I cried out with pleasure as I began to ride him.

'Brigitte was facing me and she leaned forward so that our breasts rubbed together. Then she suddenly grabbed and screamed as George brought her off with his tongue. He jerked his hips up hard and I felt his jism splash against the walls of my pussy. When he had finished I rolled off him and Brigitte scrambled down to lick his cock clean.'

Josie paused and smiled wolfishly when she noticed that wet beads of perspiration had appeared on Bernard's forehead whilst she had been speaking. She smoothed her hands over her bare breasts. 'I've made myself all hot and bothered by talking so much. Why don't you get undressed and we'll get into the mood for tomorrow?'

She pushed him back onto the bed and in a trice their bodies were fused into one eager, sensual tangle of limbs. Soon both were totally naked and Bernard closed his eyes as he devoured the sensuous feel of Josie's cool fingers caressing his scrotum. She moved her wrist upwards to twirl her fingertips inside his thatch of dark pubic curls.

He panted with suspense as Josie's hand moved over his throbbing tool without touching it. Her little finger sought out the tiny rivulet of smooth skin between his hair and the root of his prick.

'Lie back and relax, I want to ride you,' whispered the aroused girl as she pushed his head gently back onto the pillow. She swung herself above him, letting the Dane capture one erect tawny nipple in his mouth as, with a squeal of delight, she mounted him and impaled herself upon his rock-hard quivering cock.

Bernard growled as Josie rode faster and faster on his cock, gyrating her hips. His hands slid round to scoop up the soft fleshy cheeks of her bum as she wriggled around to work in his thick tool as far as possible inside her pussy. She bounced merrily away upon his rampant rod

171

and she cried out: 'Oh yes, yes! Keep going, Bernie, your big cock is giving my clitty such a wonderful rub!'

He gritted his teeth but the sensations of the sweet nipping of her cunny muscles were so strong that he climaxed much sooner than he would have wished inside her sticky honeypot. With his cock vibrating in a fierce spasm of joy, he arched his back upwards and flooded her love channel with hot creamy spunk.

'Aaaagh! I'm there too!' Josie screamed and thrust her lithe body on top of him, rubbing her nipples against his chest as she too exploded into a body-wrenching orgasm.

After they had recovered, Bernard slid out of bed. As he covered her body with the duvet, he said: 'I'm just going to the bathroom, don't go away, I'll be back in a minute.'

'I'm not going anywhere,' she replied sleepily and he nodded with satisfaction and then bent down to kiss her forehead saying: 'I'm glad to hear that for I'd love you to stay the night – after all, there's little point in your leaving now and coming back again here early in the morning.'

Josie looked up at him and gave a tiny smile. 'Thanks, Bernard, a good fuck and now a good night's sleep – what more can any girl want?'

Bernard Jensen was an early riser and it was only minutes after half-past six in the morning when his eyes fluttered open after seven hours of deep, restful slumber. As usual, he woke up with a raging erection and although Josie lay on her side beside him with her back pressed against his chest, with great difficulty he resisted the temptation to slide his tool into the cleft between her dimpled buttocks. He needed any fucking today to take place in front of the camera.

However, when Josie stirred and felt his throbbing tool pulsating against her bottom, she reached round and slicked her hand up and down his hot, velvet-skinned shaft.

'No, we must get up, we've a long day ahead,' he gasped but with a throaty gurgle she dived down and began licking his cock from top to base whilst Bernard took a deep breath and breathlessly continued: 'I mean it, Josie, we can have some fun together after work.'

But his resistance started to crumble when the tip of her wet tongue flickered around the ultra-sensitive area just behind his scrotum. He surrendered unconditionally when she opened her lips and somehow managed to stuff his entire ballsack into her mouth. She grabbed his palpitating prick with both hands as she released his balls and began to nibble and suck along the barrel of his thick eight-inch boner.

'You naughty girl,' Bernard panted as she slicked her fist up and down his shaft whilst swirling her tongue along the top of his smooth uncapped helmet. But Josie simply looked up at him and gave him a sly wink whilst she proceeded to fuck Bernard's sated shaft with her suctioning mouth, swiftly establishing a slow sensuous rhythm by bobbing her tousled head up and down as she gradually drew in more and more of his polished veiny truncheon between her lips.

And as she sucked him, she toyed with his tightening balls through the soft wrinkled skin of his hairy pink scrotum. This soon set Bernard off and, with an enormous shudder, he sent a huge wad of salty jism down her throat which she gulped down greedily, licking up every last droplet as she milked his cock until it shrivelled into limpness inside her mouth.

'Now what were you saying?' she enquired cheekily, but the Dane was unable to reply, although he wagged his finger at her in reproof as he lay on his back, his chest heaving as he fought to regain his composure.

'You could at least bring me off in another way if your cock isn't up to it,' Josie added reproachfully, and Bernard groaned, for there were several bits and pieces of work he wanted to clear up before breakfast. On the other hand, he needed to keep Josie in the right mood for the orgy scene he had planned, so spent though he was, he wordlessly grasped her jouncy bum cheeks and pulled them down until she was actually sitting on his face.

Josie squealed as he buried his lips inside her succulent moist honeypot, searching out the tangy love nectar with his tongue. Her clitty was already peeking out between her cunny lips and he sucked in the rubbery nub, titillating her love button with the tip of his fluttering tongue.

Like Marc and Pierre, Belinda Blisswood's French friends, Bernard was an adept cunnilinguist and Josie's full-throated cries of excitement soon echoed around the room as he ran his wicked tongue lightly along the edges of her slit. She wriggled wildly as he jabbed the tip into the puckered whorl of her arse-hole.

Then Bernard attacked her cunt again, his tongue darting in and out of her juicy crack so forcefully that Josie imagined that she was being properly fucked by his proud stiffstander. He turned his attention back to her swollen clitty, teasing the flesh with his teeth which set Josie on course to a florious finish. Deep, powerful tremors rumbled through her body and then she yelled with happiness and a veritable stream of love juice flowed out of her cunt all over Bernard's face as she bucked to and fro in the throes of a truly magnificent climax.

At half past nine, a fleet of three taxis rolled into the carriageway of Millchurch Cottage which Bernard had rented for the weekend. The owner, Falmington-On-Sea's randy MP, Sir Stafford Stiffkey, had no idea of the identity of the people who had signed the rental agreement with his agent.

Bernard had fretted until Christine and Mandy, the two strippers from London had turned up at the hotel, but he relaxed when he saw the two girls arrive with Harry, a handsome, softly spoken West Indian, who had driven them down to Falmington straight from their last performance at a private gentleman's club in St James's Street. Everyone else had arrived at the Berkeley on time and so far all had gone according to plan. When they had decamped from the taxis, the cast filed into the cottage and Bernard assembled them in the lounge and announced his plan of action. 'Okay everyone, listen carefully please,' he began. 'The storyline this morning is quite straightforward and I'd like to start shooting in five minutes' time.'

He turned to one of the pretty strippers and said: 'Chrissie, you play the bored housewife who's just come home from a hard morning's work filling your trolley at the local supermarket. You're all hot and bothered so you strip off and go into the bathroom to cool off.'

'Fine, I really could do with a shower. There wasn't time to have one after the last show at Glynn's, was there, Mandy?' said the coltish brunette who was perched on the arm of the sofa opposite Kent Bailey, the eighteen-year-old student who had answered Bernard's advertisement in the evening paper. Her green mini-dress barely stretched over her lap and the sight of her smooth bronzed thighs was already causing a stir in the young man's groin.

'No, though it was quite a night, wasn't it? Crikey, I've never seen Johnny Gewirtz let his hair down like that before,' chirped up her colleague, an equally attractive girl in her mid-twenties.

Belinda, Sharon and Josie had been gossiping quietly

together in the corner but mention of the name of this well known actor who was known throughout Britain for his role as a surgeon in the popular TV soap opera *Ask Doctor Valerie* made the girls prick up their ears.

'*The* John Gewirtz?' asked Belinda and Mandy nodded and answered: 'Yeah, I don't think London's big enough for more than one! Do you know what that crazy bugger did – Mike Glynn had booked two beautiful French birds to do a double act and whilst they were undressing each other, Johnny ran on to the stage and joined in!'

'Gosh, that must have put the cat among the pigeons,' said Belinda with interest. 'Did they have to drag him off the stage?'

'In the end,' chuckled Chrissie. 'What happened was that he got over-excited when the girls slipped off each other's blouses. Neither of them were wearing anything underneath and you could almost hear the punters gasp as they flaunted their tits at the audience. The girls were naked except for tiny white bikini briefs and I was standing at the back of the club when I heard Mike Glynn say: "Well Johnny, how would you like to be the meat in that sandwich? Wouldn't it be great to have the blonde girl suck your cock and the brunette lick your balls before you fuck them?"

"Chance would be a fine thing," he muttered back and Mike teased him, saying that even if the girls were willing, he would bet a tenner that Johnny wouldn't have the nerve to stand up and shag the girls in public.

'I found out later that Johnny had won six hundred quid at the Victoria Sporting Club earlier on but anyhow, he pulled out a thick wad from his pocket and said to Mike: "Put your money where your mouth is, Mike. Make it a hundred quid and you're on."

"Done," said Mike promptly and he called out something in French to the girls, who nodded their heads.

Before you could say Jack Robinson the audience were on their feet cheering on Johnny Gewirtz who was out there in the spotlight tearing off his clothes. When he got down to his Y-fronts, the brunette stopped him from going any further by putting her hand on his arm and making him sit down on a chair which they had brought on stage. Then she tugged down her own bikini bottom and showed us all her hairy pussy mound. Next thing, she swung round to Johnny and pulled his pants down over his colossal hard-on so that he sat bollock naked with his cock sticking up between his legs whilst Mike Glynn came out from the side of the stage and popped Johnny's discarded clothes into a large carrier bag.'

'Sounds as if the spectators had their money's worth,' commented Josie and now Mandy took up the story and went on: 'I should say so, even the band stopped playing to watch what Johnny Gewirtz was going to do. They didn't have long to wait because the other girl had now also rolled down her panties. She dropped to her knees in front of him stark naked, facing the audience so we could see her love lips pouting out of her little blonde bush of pussy hair.

'Meanwhile, the brunette sat on his knee, sliding her hand up and down his tadger whilst the blonde girl began to lick his balls and everyone roared with laughter when Johnny panted out loud: "I don't believe this! I'll wake up in a minute and find out it's all a dream!"

"It's no dream, just don't forget to get your hundred quid from Mike Glynn," called out one of his friends who was sitting near the front. The brunette splayed her legs for Johnny to plunge three of his fingers into her cunt, running them inside her cunny in a kind of circular motion which drove her wild.

'We could see his gleaming cock see-sawing out of her squelchy pussy whilst she tossed her head from side to side as she jiggled up and down on his tool. She said something in French to the blonde bird who squeezed Johnny's balls and jetted his jizz inside her friend's cunt.'

Katie Summerfield had been listening intently to his anecdote whilst she was setting up her camera and she remarked with a laugh: 'I don't think I'll never be able to watch *Ask Doctor Valerie* again! Mind, I've read too many stories about Johnny Gewirtz in the papers to be really shocked.'

Bernard clapped his hands and called for silence. 'Well, I hope that story has got you all in the mood. Chrissie, I've set up the camera in the bathroom. We'll begin in there – I suggest you go in there in your bra and knickers carrying a radio. Then when you're in the bath, I want Sharon to come in and talk to you.'

He turned to the blonde girl and went on: 'Sharon, you're Chrissie's best friend and you've come in to tell her about the fabulous fuck you've just had with Mark, the young window cleaner – Kent, that's you, of course – and we'll take it from there.'

'Suppose I can't think of anything to say?' asked Sharon with a worried look but the Danish director reassured her. 'Don't worry, Chrissie will lead you on. Have a quick chat with her whilst I fill the bath and check the sound equipment.' Bernard walked briskly towards the bathroom.

Chrissie whispered some advice to Sharon as she stripped off her dress and three minutes later he called out that he was ready and when he called out: 'Action!' she picked up a small transistor radio, switched it on and skipped gaily into the bathroom.

Once inside and moving her hips to the music, Chrissie played with the elastic band of her knickers, pulling it away from her belly and then slapping it back. Then with a practised saucy wiggle, she slipped out of her panties one leg at a time so that when she lifted one leg and then the second Bernard pointed the camera directly at the glossy thatch of pussy hair in the vee of her pubic mount between her thighs.

Then Chrissie remembered that her bra was still on and she reached round to unhook it and let the straps fall lazily off her shoulders. Through the viewfinder, Bernard glued his eyes to her superb uptilted breasts. She smiled as she tweaked her large raspberry-red nipples, massaging and tweaking the rubbery buds until they were fully erect.

She slid her fingers down towards the thick hirsute bush at the base of her belly and she looked up at the camera and said: 'I wonder if Freddie would be more passionate if I shaved my muff – my friend Melissa told me that her old man has been fucking her night and day since she made her cunt a shaven haven.'

Chrissie slipped into the bath and lay in the warm water which she splashed around her hairy quim as she mused: 'I'll ask Sharon, my next door neighbour. She's coming over soon for a cup of coffee and I'll see what she says – not that she has to worry, the lucky girl. Her husband Dave's a very good fuck, but he has to go travelling round the country for three nights a week. On the other hand, she's not short of cock. Hilary down the road says that she's seen Sharon plating the postman before now and I'm pretty sure she's also knocking off young Mark, that good-looking lad who took over old Mr Osborne's window-cleaning round last month.'

With a sigh she began to soap herself down but then she said out loud: 'Oooh, just thinking about Sharon and Mark is making me feel randy. I can just imagine that boy's thick prick sliding in and out of her lovely wet cunt.'

And as she spoke, Chrissie parted the soft folds of her own pussy with a questing finger and slowly started to rub herself off. She separated the puffy love lips and then her forefinger was joined by two more as she closed her eyes and frigged herself up to a state of growing excitement, wiggling her fingers inside her juicy crack. With the other hand she twiddled her erect raspberry nipples, faster and faster until she breathed hard and a cascade of love juice spouted out of her cunt and dribbled down into the bath water.

For some fifteen seconds, she lay back in the bath with a dreamy smile on her face listening to the music from her radio, but then she hauled herself up as she heard Sharon shout: 'Coo-ee, Chrissie, are you up there?'

'Is that you Sharon? Come upstairs, I'm in the bath,' Chrissie shouted back as she sat up. She made no attempt to cover herself but simply called out for Sharon to come in. A few seconds later the pretty young blonde girl knocked on the door.

'Hi Sharon, where have you been?' said Chrissie as she lathered her generous breasts with a soapy sponge. 'I thought you were coming with me to Tesco's this morning.'

'Well I was,' replied Sharon, trying hard not to giggle as she remembered the sketchy outline of the story Chrissie had suggested to her. 'But the window cleaner came round early and so I needed to stay home and make him a cup of coffee.'

Chrissie pretended to look shocked and said: 'Sharon, you naughty girl. Everyone round here knows that you've been giving young Mark more than a cup of tea? What would your old man say if he found out?'

Sharon looked blankly at her for a moment and then entering the spirit of the charade, she suddenly gained inspiration and answered: 'Oh, Dave wouldn't mind, he's very broad-minded. In fact, between you and me it really turns him on to hear me tell him how I screw other men whilst he's away. He's always hinting how he would love to watch me being shagged by another guy.'

'I don't know whether my old man would feel that way,' said Chrissie doubtfully as she splashed some warm water over her breasts. 'Mind you, I couldn't half do with a good poke, Sharon. These days Reggie is only giving me a good going-over on Saturday nights.'

'You're only getting fucked once a week?' said Sharon, clapping her hand to her cheek in horror. 'That's not enough for a lusty lady like you. For heaven's sake, why don't you get yourself a bit on the side like me – and come to think of it, you can start right now.'

She sat herself down on the edge of the bath and added: 'You see, love, I've come round to ask you for a little favour. The decorator's just arrived to finish off some work Dave's having done in our spare room and Mark and I would be awfully grateful if you would let us use one of your bedrooms for an hour or so. If you wanted him to shag you, I know that Mark would be happy to oblige!'

Chrissie frowned as she pretended to think hard about this question but then she gave a hoarse chuckle and said: 'Well, why not? You two get started and I'll join you when I've dried myself.'

Sharon's face brightened as she leaned over and giving Chrissie a kiss she said: 'Oh thanks, darling, you really are a good friend.'

Before Chrissie could reply, Bernard yelled: 'Cut! Well done, girls, that was terrific. Now you can take a short break whilst I set up again in the next room. Mr Teplin, perhaps you could give me a hand to get the camera set up in the bedroom.'

Whilst the two men helped to wheel the movie camera out of the bathroom, Katie Summerfield adjusted the focus on her Hasselblad and purred: 'Chrissie, could you just pose for a few stills please?'

'Sure,' replied the gorgeous girl as she hauled herself out of the bath and sat on the edge with just a soft green towel draped around her shoulders. She parted her legs to display her pussy which was pink and wet not only from the water but from her previous frigging. The damp curls of hair provided little cover for the open crimson chink between her spread lips.

'Very good, love,' called out Katie and gave some further instructions to her model as the camera shutter clicked. 'Now toss your head from side to side and think sexy. Yes, that's right, tweak your titties so they stand up, great, keep looking at the camera, that's fantastic!'

She moved forward to zoom in on Chrissie's pussy and went on: 'Now spread your cunny lips and open up your funnel, think of Harry's big black cock which you'll be seeing later today. Mandy told me that you've never been fucked by Harry before, so think of it filling you up. It's a hell of a size, she says, at least nine inches and so thick that most girls can't get their fingers around it!'

Chrissie now plunged her fingers deep inside her love channel and Katie's camera kept clicking away whilst she called out: 'Think of that huge prick filling you up, yes, go on, stroke your clitty, that's terrific.'

Chrissie's fingers were now a blur as with a husky cry she brought herself off as Katie took her final shots. 'Okay, Chrissie thanks very much,' she said. As Chrissie finished drying herself, Bernard came in and announced she should walk into the bedroom where Sharon and Mark were already getting down to business with a vengeance.

'Action!' yelled out Bernard and Chrissie pulled open the bedroom door. A wide grin spread over her face as she was greeted by the sight of Sharon lying face down on the bed with a large cushion stuffed under her tummy and with her hips and rounded backside stuck high in the air.

On his knees behind her, also completely nude in his role as Mark, the teenage window cleaner, was the slim figure of the eighteen-year-old Kent Bailey whose cock was jammed between Sharon's luscious bum cheeks and whose hands were fondling her firm uptilted breasts.

'Goodness me, what's going on here?' called out Chrissie and Sharon turned her head and gasped: 'Well, I don't really have to tell you, do I? Oooh, that's right, Mark push it in a bit more. He's got a lovely thick cock, Chrissie, much bigger than Dave's. Better still, for a youngster, he certainly knows how to use it! You'll soon see that for yourself. Now come on, Mark, fuck the arse off me!'

The fresh-faced young man coloured slightly as he smiled at Chrissie but he continued to fuck Sharon doggie-style, slewing his blue-veined truncheon to and fro in the tight cleft between her buttocks as he reamed out her juicy crack. Then at the blonde girl's urging he increased the pace of his fucking. Her bottom smacked enticingly against his slender boyish thighs as he pounded away and Sharon thrashed wildly around in sheer delight at the thrilling sensations afforded by his steel-hard shaft inside her cunt.

Chrissie's pussy also began to tingle as she watched Mark's cock sliding sensuously into Sharon's sticky honeypot, especially when the girl reached behind her and grabbed his swinging hairy ballsack as it slapped against her rump. Sensing the signal that she was ready and waiting for his climax, the lad further increased the speed of his pumping and croaked: 'Here it comes, Sharon, it's all for you!' His lean torso went rigid and his twitching tool gushed out a fountain of frothy spunk into her seething slit.

Sharon yelped with glee as her body shuddered with

the force of her own orgasm. She twisted her bum from side to side to draw out the last drains of jism from the youth's quivering cock before he collapsed on top of her.

'Wow, what a wonderful fuck! Well done, Kent, I came three times before you spunked,' she panted, rolling the boy onto his back and giving his limp wet shaft a friendly rub as she said to Chrissie: 'Oh dear, I hope you're not in too much of a hurry for a fuck. I think Kent's going to need some time to recover.'

'Cut! Okay, good work, you three,' called out Bernard and then he swivelled round to the chunky West Indian who had been standing behind him. 'Are you ready, Harry? Remember, you're the decorator from next door who needs to ask Sharon a question.'

He turned back to the girls and said: 'But when he comes back, he sees the pair of you having it away with the window cleaner and of course you invite him to make up a foursome.'

Bernard was about to continue when a white-faced Bruce Teplin came scurrying in from the hallway. 'Mr Jensen, you'd better come quickly. A car has just pulled up outside the front door.'

Who the blazes can that be, Bernard wondered as he strode out to find out who these unexpected visitors could be. Outside, Sir Stafford Stiffkey M.P. fumbled in his pocket for the front door key, blissfully unaware of what was taking place inside his cottage. He turned to the pretty girl he had met at the Sussex Conservative Association Summer Fête the previous day and said: 'What a pleasure to get away from all those people, Fiona. At least here we'll have the chance to be alone together.'

TO BE CONTINUED IN SUMMER SCHOOL 4: UP AND UNDER